BABY GEISHA

TRINIE DALTON

TWO DOLLAR RADIO
Books too loud to ignore

TWO DOLLAR RADIO is a family-run outfit founded in 2005 with the mission to reaffirm the cultural and artistic spirit of the publishing industry.

We aim to do this by presenting bold works of literary merit, each book, individually and collectively, providing a sonic progression that we believe to be too loud to ignore.

ISBN: 978-0-9832471-0-4
Library of Congress Control Number: 2011943111

Cover drawing: *Flask* by Xylor Jane
Author photograph: Jason Frank Rothenberg

Stories in this collection were also published as follows:
"Jackpot (I)" in *H.O.W. (Helping Orphans Worldwide)*; "Jackpot (II)" in Luna Luna exhibition catalog (Nothing Moments); "Baby Geisha" in *Swink*; "War Foods" in *Santa Monica Review*; "The Perverted Hobo" in Birthing Valley of the Blood Poppies exhibition catalog; "Escape Mushroom Style" in *The Lifted Brow* (Australia), *Numéro Cinq*, The Corresponding Society chapbook series; "Word Salad" in *Opium*; "Millenium Chill" in *Indiana Review*; "Shrub of Emotion" in *Ecotone*; "Wet Look" in *Puerto del Sol*; "Scarlet Gilia" in *Supermachine*; "Hairpin Scorpion" in *New Planes Public Press* (Australia); "Small Time Spender" in *Knee-Jerk Offline*, Vol. 2.

Typeset in Garamond, the best font ever.
Printed in the United States of America.

TWO DOLLAR RADIO
Books too loud to ignore

www.TwoDollarRadio.com
twodollar@TwoDollarRadio.com

BABY GEISHA

TRINIE DALTON

CONTENTS

WET LOOK

Iggy's thirty-fifth year had been all about Being Here Now, thanks to the book he'd read profiling the counterculture man who turned from acidhead to yogi in a blink. He'd interpreted this to mean, at various points, *Do what I want right here right now*, if in a hedonistic, self-destructive mood; *I miss you and I want you to be here now*, if missing his ex; *Feel my body now*, during aroused moments, and, most true to the cause, *Maybe I do have a god-source, where is it, I need it right now*. He hadn't received any spiritual clues yet and therefore planned a deluxe Be Here Now package for summer, beginning with regular detoxifying lemon-cayenne cleanses and a high-protein, low-carb steak and salad diet.

While Iggy longed to take his health to the next level on a pilgrimage to India, all he could afford was a $3-a-night campsite in the Missouri Ozarks, where he'd heard of a dolomite canyon that hosted annual gospel choirs. He wanted to hear that country mountain singing, in case divine vibes might absolve him of the skepticism he'd been schlepping around like a suitcase with a broken zipper, dropping bits of his bitter aggregate, his heavy thoughts, everywhere he went. He buzzed his red hair and read a few more books on Buddhism to prep for the trip, aching to bury complaints about his life's sequence of events in the Ozarks. The regional potential for Christianity didn't bother him as much as it used to, since the Dalai Lama said that all religions aim towards goodliness. Meeting some Christians would be wise in comparison to assuming complete strangers were self-righteous and petty. It was small-minded of him to criticize Christians when he hardly knew any and certainly had never spent more than 24 hours in the Bible belt.

After driving four days from California, across the Southwest and up through Oklahoma, Iggy selected a campsite on the banks of Missouri's Meramec, a gentle river whose ochre, chert-lined shores are hard and sharp in parts and velvety-smooth elsewhere. The chert hunks reminded Iggy of humongous camel teeth: the gorge was a dynamic, tawny experience. Many of the sedimentary chips resembled arrowheads, lending his temporary meditative landscape a tribal feeling. He pitched his tent and frivolously ambled away his first two afternoons on his patch of beach, slamming river stones together like a caveman. Some of these chert flecks housed dainty geodes with sparkling quartz crystal veins. He tended his rockhound hands, palms bruised from crushing rocks, in the aqua medicinal water. Both evenings he lined his lair's perimeter with mineral scores, ate simply—ramen and cans of beans—and did some zazen. Iggy had a week until the concert and planned to sit with his rock collection in the meantime.

As usual, his monkish plans went awry when he tired of pinto beans and craved a can of beer. Late afternoon on the third day he drove to the nearest diner, bought some French fries to eat while skimming the local paper's Crime Blotter, then stopped in the corner market for a beverage to make roughing it more palatable. Iggy was surprised to find that the convenience store had some apparently elaborate hook-up with Chinese importers, as he perused an immense collection of pyrotechnic supplies and fireworks. Way more variety in this remote store than in the Chinatowns on either coast. He selected some neon sparklers, smoke bombs that looked like mini-Navy submarines, and a Chinese lantern whistler and laid them on the counter.

"Best selection I've ever seen," Iggy said, exhilarated.

"We like fireworks up here," the clerk said. She looked to

be about twenty, had a mullet jelled back with extremely stiff curling-iron bangs jutting forward, heavy green glitter eyeliner, and wore a sleeveless black t-shirt that said *DON'T ASK ME*. The muddy car out front must have been hers.

"Any fireworks displays coming up?" Iggy asked, in opposition to the t-shirt's imperative. "I'm camping on the river for the week, getting a little stir crazy."

"Not officially," the merchant said, handing Iggy his change and goods. "But my brother is always practicing in our yard. He hopes to go pro."

"Is he practicing tonight?" Iggy asked. "I'd tag along, if I could. I'll bring a couple sixers."

"Probably is," she said. "I'll mention to him your wanting to come." The girl jotted an address down, described the dubious rural directions, and told Iggy to arrive just after dark. Iggy had a good feeling about the invitation.

"Ig," he said, extending his hand. "Short for Iggy. See you tonight."

"Jody," the girl said, shaking back with an iron grip. "We'll party." Jody smirked, and Iggy interpreted it to mean that they were going to get tanked. This was great, a date with the locals. Iggy headed back out to his campsite to river-bathe and change into clean clothes with the remaining sunlight.

As he put clean underwear on, he had no intention of showing them to Jody; it was more to boost his spirits and to enhance any impending camaraderie. His dad used to say that a person should always wear clean undergarments in case of a car accident. Otherwise, if ambulance technicians had to strip you, they might assume you're a dirty bird. Iggy hated himself for bowing down to this kid mentality, for allowing his dad's chiding voice into his head while preparing for a night out. But there he was after having scrubbed with castile soap, suds already downstream, self-consciously pulling crisp checkered boxers on inside his tent. *Thanks dad*, he thought, next pulling on his jeans, *for making me into a self-conscious wimp*. For a second, he even felt victimized by the whole of Western Society, after all, because it had dictated that father teach son to wear clean underwear at all costs. He was so middle class. *The real issue*, Iggy thought as he zipped his fly and combed his hair, *is our ill society, the barriers we build between ourselves*. Then, he remembered that he hated constantly doubting himself, his inner critic. Underwear has nothing to do with sociological barriers. Why couldn't he just pull a damn pair of boxers on without feeling so conflicted?

"This is exactly why I came out here," he said to himself, inhaling the humid Ozark air, tying his bootlaces proudly, as if shooting off fireworks with strangers might cure his fears of being wrongly judged, and in turn, cure his own ineffable judgments. Judge not lest ye be judged. That was Christian, and it made lots of sense.

Jody's house was easy to find on County Road MM because it was dark, and he saw shimmering rainbows cascading up and down over the property. Nobody left porch lights on in these hills, and the moon, tonight a tiny, insignificant sliver, was waning towards the end of its cycle. Iggy followed the display and pulled up under a green and purple spark shower.

"Howdy," he said, for the first time in his life. He was toting a case of beer as proof of ready participation.

Jody said hello then walked him over to her brother, who was lighting the fuse on a gargantuan tower called The Big One. He lit it, then took a few quick steps back before acknowledging Iggy's presence.

"Hey," he said, offering an even stronger grip than Jody's had been. "I'm Kitty." They all paused to listen to a tense bursting whistle followed by a silver explosion.

Funny name, Iggy thought. Kitty's buff, hairy arms were covered in modern primitive tattoos, and he too wore a sleeveless black tee, but it said, *DON'T HATE ME BECAUSE I'M BEAUTIFUL*. The siblings must have purchased them in tandem. Iggy wanted to tell Kitty that he liked the shirt's irony, but thought he'd better take it easy until he understood Kitty's humor better. He handed the beers to Kitty, and Kitty nodded with approval. With this, the newly forged pal trio fired up a variety show while polishing off several cans of beer.

Tastes and preferences guided Jody and Iggy's first line of conversation while Kitty worked the display.

"I noticed you went for the smallest fireworks earlier," Jody said, initiating the chat.

"They're illegal in California," Iggy said. "I thought I better keep it simple."

"California?" Jody asked. "I thought they went crazy there on Cinco de Mayo."

"Southern Cali is one giant fire hazard," Iggy said. "And honestly, I enjoy small displays as much as the fancy ones."

Iggy realized this was an unpopular view, as he'd noticed that there were no sissy smoke bombs, worms, or sparklers on-hand in this household. Every firecracker in site was titanic, cylindrical, and erect; Iggy had entered a fervent penis world, much more macho than his own more tender universe. *Dudes blow each other's cocks up all night*, he thought snidely, *get wasted, then stumble in to say their prayers*. He assumed that Kitty and Jody were Christians, due to region, but again, he caught himself making assumptions and aimed to halt this. Judging these firework displays, much less making immature, sweeping judgments against Christians who kindly invited him over, just minutes after arrival: geesh. He cursed himself and attempted to decontaminate his brain. *Love thy neighbor*, *Buddha compassion*, *it's all the same*, he generalized, continuing to talk with Jody about California versus Missouri.

Just then a snapping turtle ambled across the dirt driveway, through the obnoxious sirens of a Whistling Pete.

"That turtle must be deaf," Iggy shouted, putting his fingers in his ears.

Once Kitty spotted it, it was doomed. "Kill it!" Kitty yelled, and the siblings brutally kicked the turtle back and forth like a football until its head and legs were hanging limply from its shell. Iggy almost barfed, but didn't feel he could intervene mid-violence for fear of Kitty's backlash.

"Why'd you kill him?" Iggy asked sternly, post-mortem, as he and Jody stared down at the dead turtle illuminated by yet another firework Kitty had already walked a few paces away to blast.

"You ever been bit by a snapping turtle?" Jody asked. Iggy had not.

"He was just trying to walk over to that pond," Iggy said, pointing to the side yard. "He was probably going to lie down by his wife."

"Turtles don't have wives," Jody said, kicking dirt over where streaks of turtle blood marked the ground. Kitty sauntered over from pyro headquarters a few feet away.

"What's all this shit about turtle marriage?" Kitty asked, and the siblings laughed.

"Iggy claims that turtle had a wife," Jody said to Kitty, elbowing him to ad lib from there.

"That punk turtle probably had AIDS anyway," Kitty said.

Seriously? Iggy thought. He could have foreseen minor aggression, sure, or maybe some pinhead cousins emerging from the basement, but AIDS jokes? These people were morons. Iggy had lost several friends to AIDS, had gone to the community clinic to get tested himself more than once, and thought it was far from humorous.

"You and your AIDS have a good night then," Iggy said, stomping towards the car.

"Aw, come on," Jody said, following Iggy to his car door as

he opened it and sat down in the driver's seat. "Kitty was just joking."

"The problem with people like you," Iggy said, "is that you live your hick lives and still manage to believe there's a God up there who will forgive your idiocy."

"Why bring God into this?" Jody asked.

"It looks, from my angle," Iggy said, "like you have to be pretty fucking dumb to have faith, and that's why I don't have any." Iggy reclined in his seat, rectified but dizzy from alcohol, thrust his key into the ignition, and started the engine. He didn't care what he said at this point, or if he provoked a fight.

"So, you're too smart for God," Jody said. "Too pompous to believe in him and above hanging out with the low-lifes who do."

Iggy had not put the car in reverse yet, because he was really drunk. Some part of him, too, was still remotely interested in how the fight would play out. The scenario in which he got his ass kicked as badly as the turtle's had something heroic in it.

"You're too smart for your own good," Jody said. "That's the only tragedy here." Iggy's chest hurt, because he knew Jody was right. He tasted sour vomit in the back of his throat.

"It was obnoxious to kill that turtle," Iggy said, trying to parse out the original offense. "How can you reconcile God with cruelty like that?"

"If you really want to know," Jody said, "cut that motor. You're too loaded to drive." Kitty, in the meantime, had gone back to sorting what looked like the grand finale: ten fountains alternating with M-80s, to be lit in succession.

Was that poor turtle's death God in a hideous costume?

Jody led Iggy into their kitchen, opened a drawer in a desk occupying the breakfast nook, and handed Iggy a photo of a mashed-up car. She turned a ceiling fan on and Iggy noticed under the light that she'd changed her eyeliner color from green to blue, and had obviously re-made her face for the evening. Jody lit up a cigarette and offered one to Iggy. He took it although he didn't smoke.

"'84 Mustang," Jody said, bowing her head. "I wrapped it around a tree."

"I'm sorry," Iggy said.

"Barely survived," Jody said, then proceeding to chronicle the details leading up to her gruesome crash, including everything from the suicidal thoughts that compelled her to build a 30-beer tall Wizard Staff as part of a drinking game by which you tape empties together into a staff before battling dragons, a.k.a. liquor shots, until the Wizard topples or triumphs—to remembering the tree slam and her face, bloody and upside down, in the rear-view.

"Fourteen broken bones later," Jody said, "I was in a body cast for two months."

Midway through the story, Iggy became suspicious: Jody had had a near-death experience when she found God. *Oh no*, Iggy thought. *Next, she'll bust out the Bible tract.* But he listened, again cutting his judgment off at the pass to make way for remote sympathy. He wanted someone, by whatever means necessary, to crack open his hard shell. If he couldn't empathize with this girl, Iggy was certainly not above her turtle-dropkicking routine.

"I almost died a few times," Iggy confessed, feeling out whether or not he should mention getting AIDS-tested for needle sharing back in the day. "Can't say I was always happy to have survived."

"Why'd you really come out here?" Jody asked, sitting down on a barstool and lighting another smoke.

"I'm going nomadic," Iggy said.

"What does that mean?" Jody asked.

"If I'm in one place, I'm missing out somewhere else," Iggy said.

"What is it you think you're missing out on?" Jody asked.

She hadn't yet pulled a tract out, and Iggy settled in. Maybe she didn't have an agenda; maybe she wasn't even Christian. He pulled up a barstool at the counter next to her. Her mullet was clean and fluffy, and her bangs had been de-plastered as if they'd been washed and brushed. She, too, was wearing a clean t-shirt and probably underwear.

"If I knew that, I wouldn't be missing it, would I?" Iggy asked rhetorically. He admired the stalwart way Jody held her cigarette, between her forefinger and thumb as if in some survivalist militia.

"All I know is that once I got that body cast sliced off with the doc's pizza cutter, I wanted to find a man to settle down and have a kid with. Life's too short," Jody said.

"I hear that," Iggy said. "The only way I can slow it down is to hijack myself to random places like this."

"This place is random!" Jody laughed. "I saw you, almost speeding off in your car, bored stiff. So, you managed to slow it down after all, good for you."

Another wave of despondence about the turtle, in the form of nausea, rushed Iggy. Maybe batting that creature back and forth had been Jody's way of slowing a moment down. It had operated as a slow-motion nightmare. Iggy couldn't help but mentally replay the event. He had burned through quite a few horror films in his time, and it crossed his mind that maybe that's what he had liked about them—the way time suspended in nascent cataclysm followed by the predicted trauma. Hell, even his past drug use was likely tied to this.

Kitty marched in to wash his charcoal-blackened fingers in the sink.

"What are you two lovebirds up to?" Kitty asked. "You missed a fine finale. Five Black Diamonds in a row. I wore sunglasses."

"We traumatized Ig with our turtle rugby," Jody said. "And I think we owe him an apology."

A sobering shock circulated through Iggy like hot coffee.

"Sorry, Miss Sensitive," Kitty said. "But you have us to thank for saving your big toe, which that turtle might have snapped clean off."

"Thanks, but I can care for my own toes," Iggy said, looking down at them, snug in hiking boots. "I'd better head out."

"Nice to meet you," Kitty said, followed by Jody. There had been no expectation to hook up, which also made Iggy feel better, as Jody was not the most attractive girl he'd ever seen. The siblings waved Iggy off, and shot one last spray up in the air to light his path down the obscure, rocky driveway to pavement.

The next day was sunny on the Meramec, and Iggy had a hangover. He decided to float. He pulled on his trunks, rented a tube, and headed out, wading off shore into deeper water flow and getting snagged along the way on Missouri's thorny equivalent to asparagus fern, the nasty plant that used to plague his childhood home's yard. Iggy wondered if his mother had named him in honor of that irritating plant, because Iggy rhymed with *spriggy* and that sounded a lot like *prickly*. Iggy's mom loved singing and rhyming like that—always the poet. Iggy then flashed back to his ex-girlfriend, Finnegan, who had claimed his name reminded her of an opera-singing bear bathing under a misty waterfall. Iggy liked that idea better, having no idea what it meant but missing Finnegan, who had left him for a woman. What could he have done about that? *All the women I fall for are lesbians,* he mused, wondering why. In fact, the very idea of lesbians aroused him on the spot, and he got a pup tent in his trunks despite the cold water as he plunged in. Too bad there were no women to be seen for miles, and that he was a total chicken when it came to propositioning them. He spinned his tube around to catch sun sparkles on the innocuous rapids. He would float all day down to another tube rental place, and shuttle back to his camp where he could jostle his pup tent in the privacy of his own larger shelter.

Iggy drifted alone for the first hour, contemplating the night before: his fury inflamed by savagery only to be tamed by a glimpse of authentic human decency, the unexpected sincerity of Jody's confession. Then, he came upon a group of people whose tubes were tied together with ropes, and who had also tied nets to their tubes as makeshift beer coolers. *Hey!* they hollered, *Float this way!*

Iggy wafted down. *Welcome!* They yelled like cheerleaders at a varsity game. *Whoo hoo! High fives!* The likely homecoming queen was not Iggy's type but was gorgeous in that wholesome midwestern way with long chestnut hair streaked blond. As she tossed him a can, Iggy caught it then dunked his head in the river, flipping his hair while forgetting that he had none.

"Where you headed, Wet Look?" she asked.

"Down to Minks Pass," Iggy said. He made small talk with the girl, holding their tubes together to stay connected. People were mostly amicable in these parts, at least, but he didn't know what it all added up to yet.

The tube crew snaked along, catching currents, hitting occasional rocks and diversifying, only to reconvene around the next bend. Twice, people flipped and everyone scrambled to get the man down back on board, a wobbly affair. Iggy rolled off his tube periodically to swim, and in shallower water he let his tube buttress his buns against boulder collisions. It was nice, this living in the present, listening to kids talk about their latest dramas without having to think back to being dumped by Finnegan, or of his parents, who he hadn't called back in six months. Iggy was the youngest in his family to have declared bankruptcy after having maxed out seven credit cards. He was avoiding a permanent address to evade creditors, really, and badly wanted a second chance but didn't know how he'd ever pay down the bills, though reduced from bankruptcy, without a decent job as opposed to the odd jobs he'd taken in recent years due to his meandering, itinerant schedule. If he stayed in one place, he'd be paying the government back into his forties. Then again, moving made it nearly impossible to meet another woman, not that he'd have the confidence to date with so much debt. He felt he had nothing to offer; he'd shaved his head to start anew but it actually made him feel even more denuded. The Wet Look nickname, ouch. All of this crossed his mind as the kids high fived and hollered, carousing until they swirled into the Minks Pass River Company's eddy spot.

"Nice floating with you!" the girl said to Iggy, releasing their tubes for independent floats to the beach. Iggy accidentally spun into some shore grasses, but pretended he was checking for river life.

Snap. Iggy yanked his foot out of the water to find the whole tip of his big toe mangled. Blood dribbled down his throbbing foot. A snapping turtle got him after all. *Fucking Meramec*, he cursed under his breath, limping ashore, dragging his raft behind him. He was often verging on lithe, soulful summer days, literally bumping up against them, but never could quite pull off a single day of carefree tranquility. *I'm out of this deadbeat place first thing tomorrow morning*, Iggy told himself. The horror of enlightenment was too painful, and all Iggy immediately craved was a beach towel and a band-aid.

MILLENIUM CHILL

Sweaters dangled from every surface. I had three maxed-out dressers, but sweaters still cascaded down everything. Sleeves were falling off my bookshelf ledges, and a sweater pile in the corner collapsed silently to the floor like a dead knitted octopus. Sweaters were shoved under the bed's covers, and they lined the bathroom towel rack. I found a sweater wedged behind the wok in the kitchen cabinet, and two were plopped on the entryway table. There were three sweaters slung over my desk chair, if I needed one while seated. Four sweaters hung on the coat rack, and one was stuffed between some couch cushions.

From any location in my house I could reach a sweater just in case. *In case of what?* I asked myself. *How many sweaters does one woman need?* I looked around my apartment and decided I'd gone crazy owning so many sweaters. There are only so many sweaters a body can pile onto itself. *Am I really that cold?* Grabbing and folding a sweater out of respect for this remarkably comfortable knittery, I peered under the bed and saw a sweater bunched up, collecting dust bunnies.

It was the middle of winter but it was time for spring-cleaning. I'm sure people who are used to winter often clean in the cold, that this is not a novel idea. But I'd never had gray skies for months straight or considered so often what to wear. I needed more sweaters than I used to. I felt like I'd just moved to Antarctica, though I'd only moved cross-country. I couldn't then bear to part with any sweaters, because their warmth reminded me of the golden sun. I drank some pomegranate juice to prep for major sweater folding.

After folding ten, I wanted an icy shot of vodka to cheers myself for surviving winter. I looked to the clock; only noon. I don't take vodka shots that early; I'm too paranoid about getting drunk in winter daytime. People in northern countries are notorious for passing winter in drunken stupors, and I don't want to fall prey. But what else is there to do, when it's dark half the year, than to toast the melancholy sky until it disappears?

I put on some Cajun music, chugged two glasses of water instead of vodka, and aimed to work until all sweaters were hidden from view. I hadn't heard Cajun music in a while, but it always gets me fired up. It made me want to sit on the porch, stare at alligators, and sweat. It sizzled. I took two aspirin with two more glasses of water. I stretched. I wanted to kill the headache induced from my noticing the sloppy sweaters. Then I put quite a few more away.

Humming along to Cajun songs, folding sweaters, and shoving them into drawers, I left the curtains tied open to let in what little daylight existed. Halfway through the job, I looked to the window and noticed an old woman staring in. She squinted, head leaning in, not quite pressing against the glass. Was she admiring my sweater collection? I went to the front door and opened it.

"Hello, ma'am," I said. She was shivering under a scrawny black shawl.

"Hello, little girl," she said, even though I am mother-aged.

"Are you okay?" I asked.

"I am cold," she moaned. "Old, and cold. Could you spare a sweater, my dear?" She had an overbite, and yellow teeth peeked over her bottom lip as she talked.

"Of course," I said. I would survive minus a sweater. "I'll be right back."

It seemed a trap. But I'd expect more a trap *taking* something from a stranger. She wasn't giving. I opened my bottom dresser drawer and chose a black one. There were three other black sweaters and, besides, this one made me look gaunt. I walked over to the door, opened it, and stepped out.

"Here you go," I said. "I hope it fits."

"Bless you, my child," she said, pulling it immediately on. I said goodbye and closed the door.

"Don't you think it's odd that I just *happened* to be putting sweaters away, and this woman peeped in and guilt-tripped me into giving her one?" I said to my best friend, Elise, on the phone the following week.

"People get cold where you live," Elise said. "There are lots of old women there who need sweaters."

I nibbled a bagel chip. "What's she doing with that sweater now?" I mused, picturing it bundled with string on a chalked-out pentagram in the dirt, deep in the woods.

"She's probably wearing it," Elise said.

"She's doing more than wearing it," I said. "Trust me."

"Call the police," Elise said. "A woman is wearing a sweater."

"Shut up," I said, noshing another chip. "I'm going to find out what she's up to."

The next day the lady returned. She peered in the same window, through light snowfall, squinting with her hand as a visor. I didn't open the door at first, but ten minutes later she still stared in. I got a grip—the worst she could do was bang my shin with her cane. I opened the door. "I'm sorry, ma'am," I said. "But I don't have anymore sweaters for you. There's a thrift store a couple blocks down."

"I don't need a sweater, dear," she said. She pulled at her black sweater sleeve, and displayed it under the shawl. "You gave me one. But I wonder if you have any bagel chips?"

"Bagel chips?" I asked. "I don't have any. The bagel store is near the thrift store," I said.

"Excuse my nosiness," she said. "But I walked by yesterday and couldn't help but notice that you were eating bagel chips while you spoke on the phone. I thought you might have a few leftover for a little old lady who's too frail to bake her own." Her long silver hair ends blew in the wind from beneath the scarf tied over her head.

Was this a joke?

"I ate them all," I said, feeling guilty for not saving her some.

"Woe is me!" she cried. "What shall I eat?"

I mentally rummaged the pantry. I didn't want anyone starving.

"I'll be right back," I said, closing the door.

The pantry contained a few sundry items that wouldn't alone make good meals. Dried beans, mustard, cardamom pods. I had two hundred sweaters but not a single can of soup. I found some pasta and took it to the door.

"Go make some spaghetti," I said to her. She snatched the noodles out of my hands.

"God bless you, my child!" she yelled, and scurried down the block. I watched her turn the corner before I shut the door.

I installed thick velvet curtains patterned with fleur-de-lys, and vowed to keep them closed until this lady chose a new begging route. I might as well have been moving into a cinderblock bunker, it would be so dark with the curtains cutting out the already dim winter light. But I couldn't have homeless people stopping by. Once the drapes were up I went outside, and I couldn't see in. Pride surged through me, sweet triumph. But back inside, staring at the fleur-de-lys repeating in diagonal rows, I felt snooty. *Keep Out Old Ladies*, fleur-de-lys say. My senile grandma came to mind. As she would have said, *What makes you so high and mighty?*

I took the curtains down. They wouldn't solve this. I'd sensed the woman's presence staring at the closed curtains from outside. I felt sorry for her; she looked so helpless. I called Elise, and after chatting, told her that the old woman might as well just move in. I'm a Yes addict. Elise said it could be worse.

"Worse than what?" I asked.

"Being homeless," Elise said.

"We're lucky, aren't we?" I asked.

My mind drifted to a week prior, when I was so naïvely putting sweaters away, singing Cajun songs, oblivious to the world of poverty and famine.

"Okay," I said. "I'll keep giving her stuff."

Elise and I hung up. Maybe Elise was in cahoots with the old woman.

I dreamed of an elephant who wore metal sandals—bronze coins strapped on. He blasted through the wall on his way into my living room, letting in cold winds that froze my cat and the houseplants. That elephant, on television, usually represents the family's drug addict or past history of abuse. I figured it was easy to analyze. The elephant sauntering through my house was thunderous and disruptive, but there was a certain novelty in having an elephant visit. Maybe it was an honor? I couldn't decide. He stuck his trunk out at me. I put a spaghetti package in it that he curled up into his mouth, plastic and all. Then I opened another package and shoved single strands of spaghetti straight up his trunk, the long way. He blinked his eyelashes, signifying pleasure. It reminded me of how boys used to stick pencils up their noses in class.

The woman showed up three days after the elephant. I went to the door and opened it; there was no use pretending. She made eye contact then glanced down at my outfit, as if deciding what item to ask for.

"Make it quick," I said. "I'm busy." She didn't need to know I had been putting butterfly stickers on a letter to Elise. My patience dwindled even though I was supposed to nurture the elephant. She squinted at me and waved her cane at something.

"Tell me what you need."

The woman had a handbag this time. She dug through it and removed a list, presumably full of necessary items.

"I don't know how I live without these few basics," she said.

At least fifty things, including potted plants, a furry pet, and several hundred sweaters. A television set. A red carpet. A tan corduroy blazer. Green galoshes. A desk. My life. Stalking me, she'd memorized my possessions.

"Go away," I said, attempting to shut the door. The woman wedged her cane into the crack.

"I will die," said the woman, "if you don't help me. It's so cold outside." She put her hands together, praying to me.

I looked at the heavy elephant-blue clouds dotting the sky. A steely wind gust blew by, and the woman shivered, even through her shawl and new sweater.

"I am not a genie," I said. "I will give you one thing off this list. Decide fast. It's too cold to stand here with the door open."

"I want your cat," she said.

"You can't have my cat," I said. "Choose something else."

"Your hands."

"They're attached to my arms."

We settled on a set of silverware and a heat lamp. As she walked away I pictured her in a warm, well-lit hovel, twirling hot spaghetti with a fork. I went inside and re-hung the curtains.

I thought drapery kept your house warm, but that night I fell asleep with the comforter pulled up over my face. Three sweaters were layered over my pajamas. My toes ached through their wool socks. In the middle of the night I got up to check the thermometer: 29 degrees. Cranking the heat hadn't helped. I wanted to shed sweaters in general but tonight I needed every one of them. Sure, this justified my sweater obsession. But I was tired of wearing so many clothes. I lay in bed with my eyes open, and my cat huddled under the covers next to my thigh to thaw.

I dozed. When I woke up the first time, I was in an ice hotel, rolling in furs. The cat was an orange tiger sleeping on a white tiger skin rug at the foot of my bed. Feline stripes coagulated into jail bars. I fell back asleep, and the next time I woke up I was a penguin, huddled en masse with millions of other penguins as blizzards threatened our bird fortress. Looking down, an egg teetered on my webbed feet, and I struggled to tuck it into my chest feathers. Claustrophobic. I passed back out. Next morning, entering the kitchen to make coffee, icicles lined the sink faucet where water had trickled. I dialed the landlady and told her the heater was broken.

It must have been a curse. The cold house was punishment for my lack of sympathy. I was going to freeze my ass off for the rest of my life in an eternally frigid hell. Contemplating this, I realized I was tied to that woman by body temperature. She was now home, in her hovel, staying toasty. My simultaneous struggle to get hot only drew us psychically closer. It's only hell if I believe it to be so. Cut the cord. I tugged at my purple pullover and set it on the kitchen counter. Then I unzipped the snowflake cardigan. The turtleneck came off, then the long-johns. Slippers kicked off, socks, and lastly my underwear, until I stood there nude. Goosebumps took over. It was the coldest I've been in this century, and the chill was magnificent.

PURA VIDA

"Sloths? I'm on it," Joanne said, hanging up with her editor. She was on the way to her bedroom, practically sprinting towards the closet door to read the travel list she kept tacked up there. Ten essentials for her valise: *Big round sunglasses, steno pad, pens, phone charger…* She made this list after discovering that Joan Didion kept one. *What Would Joan Do?* she often asked herself. This assignment entailed flying a few countries south to pet sloths, and she vowed to cover the sloth story as if her life was on the line.

Joanne had just finished a feature on Alaskan giant vegetable farming. She was proud of it, though it was no Pulitzer nominee. For it, Joanne had tracked one farmer's journey from farm plot to county fair during Alaska's short, potent growing season. During summer there, round-the-clock, steroidal sunlight makes cabbages and pumpkins, among other things, grow to the size of economy cars. This time her editor assigned her a weekend in Costa Rica, not to cover the annual Ridley Sea turtle breeding like every other sentimental glossy magazine on the planet, but to visit a sloth hospital. At the height of turtle coverage, the sloth hospital was the spin. This clinic adopted orphaned sloths, who in turn performed human therapy. Joanne's job was to discover how these sloths healed humans with their dark, charming eyes. Packing for the trip could have gone smoothly, were it not for Joanne's roommates—her two pesky sisters. They were unemployed performance artists who, at the most inopportune times, tainted Joanne's dutiful existence.

That evening, before the flight, Joanne packed toiletries in the bathroom.

"This movie's so good you don't even have to watch it!" VV yelled from the living room.

Joanne put her doll-sized bottles down to go see what was so good. But VV started playing jazzy clarinet over the film's dialogue, so Joanne couldn't tell what was happening.

"What's the film about?" Joanne asked.

VV tooted out a mellifluous but unintelligible woodwind answer.

Joanne stomped back into the bathroom to pack the hell out of her toiletries.

VV had the ethereally disjunctive habits of those drunk on bubbly. People assumed VV was an airhead but Joanne knew it was a massive cover-up. VV had choppy blond hair that frequently changed to red-brown or orange. Currently, one side of her hair was shoulder-length while the other side was shaved, like vintage Cyndi Lauper. Joanne's unwavering dark brown Didion bob dulled in comparison.

"What are you doing?" Dena called into Joanne a few minutes later, coming in from the porch stoop to watch Joanne pack.

"Getting rid of these hair brushes," Joanne said. Her toiletries were adrift in drawers crammed with her sisters' junk; it was delaying her task's completion. "Why do we have so many?"

"How many do we have?" VV called in, taking a clarinet break. Their brownstone was small and eavesdropping was inevitable.

"Just enough," Dena called back, leaning on the bathroom's doorjamb, "to…"

"Host a salon?" VV asked.

"Exactly!" Dena yelled.

"I'm throwing these out," Joanne said.

"Yeah, about that," Dena said. "We might want those brushes later."

"Actually… can I have one right now?" VV asked. At this point, VV was loitering in the doorjamb too.

Joanne slapped a brush into VV's hand. "I'm chucking the rest."

"Don't you have anything better to do than to throw our cherished possessions out, Chore Boy?" asked VV. "Why don't you try going on a date?"

Joanne rarely had luck recruiting her sisters to perform organizational tasks. Chore Boy was code that meant Joanne was passive aggressively bossy. But, Joanne figured, someone had to keep these jokers in line. Joanne was thirty, while VV and Dena were twenty-four and twenty-six, going on twelve.

"Journalism is extremely social," Joanne snapped back.

"No, it's not," Dena said. "And you don't have to write a report about us, so stop counting our brushes."

"You are not our mom," VV added, brushing her hair.

"Can we not do this now?" Joanne asked. Their ambitious mother had also been a second-rate journalist who never won her Pulitzer. The three girls agreed on one thing: that their single mom, who had taken even the lamest assignments out of financial desperation, and who, in the years before the Sexual Revolution, had voiced constant frustrations about sexist news coverage and low pay, had lived a Sisyphean existence that none of them wished to emulate. Their mom had died of a stroke, and Joanne wanted retribution in the form of major journalism awards.

The room grew sullen. Joanne pulled a drawer out of its cabinet, dumped the brushes on the floor, marched off to her bedroom, and slammed the door shut; she remained holed up until the next morning when she left without saying goodbye.

After transferring in Mexico City, Joanne rode in a ten-person plane that teetered over volcanic peaks socked in by clouds, to reach the rainforest. She thought she'd die flying straight through this thunderstorm. Lightning flashed all around her, fracturing the sky into scary gray shards. She felt two pangs of guilt for leaving the conflict unresolved back home with Sylvia and Jardina, VV's and Dena's full names. Their mother had always referred to the three girls by their full, more florid names. Joanne felt a third guilt pang, sharp as a cramp. Her sisters would never change, but they were the only family she had left.

Joanne sent loving vibes to North America from the seat of the janky plane, watching boxy, brightly painted shantytowns punctuated by palm trees whiz by below. There were seventeen species of palm here, more than anywhere else in the world, Joanne had read in the previous airplane's magazine. On this last leg of her journey, Joanne realized that she had completely neglected to research the kinds of trees sloths lounge in. She wouldn't have a clue where to look for them. *Hello, sloth journalist, is anybody in there?*

As the plane landed in a strip shaved out of banana plantation that looked like Earth's bikini wax, Joanne took notes about the setting in her spiral notebook for her first draft due in five days. As thundershowers whipped banana leaves and palm fronds into feathery green tornadoes, there were three minutes of *Heart of Darkness* effect—feeling the foreignness of the place and wondering how she'd escape alive—until Joanne remembered she had just landed in Costa Rica, a country with no military.

She secretly hoped her cell phone wouldn't work in the jungle, but she was compelled to try it and the reception was excellent. She had several work-related messages. *Joanne, call me asap.—Joanne, guess what? You've been invited to lecture on sloth healing! I've already accepted on your behalf.—Joanne, where are you? Call me back...* The speed with which her editor relayed messages seemed ludicrous at this podunk airport—two benches, a small attendant booth, a soda machine, and the one-plane landing strip. Pressure to come back with shamanic jungle revelations, wearing a sloth-claw necklace, was insinuated in these brief voicemails. What did these people expect from a woman who pets a sloth for a few minutes? Hailing a cab, she thought again of her sisters, hanging loose, probably reciting spoken-word poems to each other in a shared bubble bath. Joanne, in her own rekindled bubble bath of rage, fumed knowing this article would be paying their rent.

"*Le gusta la selva?*" the driver asked, glancing in the rear-view at Joanne. *Do you like the forest?*

As the small taxi crossed streams and rutted-out, muddy washes on the way to the lodge, Joanne glimpsed a coati, the anteater's cousin, grazing roadside. It had the same shaped head as a sloth, or wait a minute… Joanne's mind came up blank trying to picture a sloth head.

"*Sí, me gusta. Es una coati?*" She pointed out the window. *Animal knowledge is the mark of a real gentleman*, Joanne wrote on her steno pad. *Even the cab drivers here revere sloths*—It could work.

"*No sé,*" he said. "*Los rancheros no gustan estos animales sucios.*" *Ranchers don't like those dirty animals.*

She didn't understand his Spanish, and she didn't even know the Spanish word for *sloth*. Because of the hairbrushes, she'd forgotten her Spanish dictionary. She closed her notebook and gritted her teeth.

Checked in to the lodge, a series of teak buildings completely constructed on stilts, Joanne wasn't feeling the boggy central lowland rainforest. Lanky trees dripped with vines, and a trail of leaf-cutter ants marched lime green sails on their backs across her balcony railing. Maybe the ants were headed for the river a few hundred yards away, to windsurf on their leaf bits. The river behind the lodge wasn't overtly sinister but had serious undertow: glassy eddies belied vicious whirlpools. It lacked the gentle demeanor of Joanne's favorite bodies of water: upstate New York's placid lakes. Joanne increasingly lacked that gentle demeanor as well. This river malingered, its rapids looked treacherous, and its watershed was host to caymans, river otters, bats, water moccasins, winged lizards who could walk across water, spider monkeys, piranhas, tiger herons, sloths, and an occasional jaguar, among who knows what else. Nestling into her porch hammock, Joanne recalled her favorite essay, "In Bogotá," in which Didion nails overwhelming wilderness.

On the Colombian coast it was hot, fevered, eleven degrees off the equator with evening trades that did not relieve but blew hot and dusty...

Joanne, swinging, got out her steno pad to compare what she had written so far.

Sloth. What is it? We all want to know. Is it a furry mammal or one of those half-mammal half-bird animals, like a platypus? [RESEARCH SLOTH BIOLOGY]

She slugged water from a plastic bottle. She pictured herself in a tank top and walking shorts, getting hugged by cuddly bear-things with long arms. She was *so* going to get a Pulitzer for this. People in New York would not believe she got to pet sloths. Plus, the receptionist told her that Jane Goodall had worked nearby with howler monkeys. She started to feel like *una journalista auténtica.* Flipping through a field guide, she found the sloth page and tried to memorize the sloth's face shape.

"See the *tucanes*?" a man said to Joanne, after a chicken, rice, and plantains dinner in the dining hall that night. She was reclining on a chaise longue by the pool, staring up at the stars and listening to the tree frogs sing. Their chirps animated the constellations. Joanne looked into a spotlight laced with fluttering pipistrelle bats until she saw the silhouette of a black bird with a huge beak perched on a phone line.

"Chestnut-mandibled," the man said. He was wearing extremely thick glasses. How did he see a bird fifty feet up?

"*Muy bonita*," Joanne said. Maybe it could be romantic...

except that this man looked like a mole. Joanne wondered if his eyes could swivel 360 degrees, like a chameleon's—it would make some sense in this region.

Joanne hadn't dated anyone since Basil, who acted more like a bartender than a high-powered professional. Joanne had trouble meeting someone to co-write articles, to read her works aloud to, a lover who could edit her sentences. It was so fucked up, but she could only relate to people through work. She remembered a distant time when she could identify with all types. As a child, Joanne had despised watching her mother slog through daily existence as a lonely matron. She wondered what she still had in common with non-journalists. Maybe this rainforest expert would show her.

"Are there more *tucanes* here?" Joanne asked, pronouncing toucans like he did, in flirty Spanish plural.

"*Sí*," said the man, handing her a flashlight. "*Soy Raphael. Mucho gusto.*"

The chestnut-mandibled, a showy toucan with a brown-striped beak, gave Joanne and Raphael, the myopic birder, a happy send-off onto the trails. Raphael took Joanne for a flashlight tour of the bushes to look for *serpentes* and *insectos.* Joanne preferred the hand-sized luna moths that flew erratically towards her light beam, and the strawberry dart frogs that looked like single red-painted fingernails. Also impressive were these walnut-sized seedpods ravaged with teeth marks.

"They're the monkey's favorite meal," Raphael said, winking at Joanne as if monkey food was his big turn-on.

That would have been the makeout cue, but Joanne exuded a bitter DEET sweat, her hair was plastered to her neck from humidity, and she didn't feel vampish at all covered in mosquito bites. Joanne was so far from feeling sexy that this night-walk was quickly growing tedious.

"Look!" Raphael shout-whispered. He pointed his light at a walking stick, a foot-long insect twig look-alike. It crawled off along the teak-planked footpath. The walking stick became oddly phallic in Joanne's mind, perhaps because it was the first long object they'd seen.

"Want to see my hammock?" she asked. Raphael nodded. They rushed back to her hut where Raphael turned off his flashlight. She fucked him quickly, not in the hammock but in her bed. At least they were lying down. She didn't feel like sharing her hammock. Joanne asked Raphael to leave as he was buttoning his pants.

Waking up feeling jaded, Joanne groggily stared at a pair of charming parrot portraits striped by sunlight leaking through the slatted window blinds. Raphael's penis was burned on her mind, small, warm, and flaccid like a freshly killed snake. *New York has ruined me*, she thought. *I'm impossible to impress.* So what if Raphael's penis looked more like a deceased baby boa than a live daddy? Dragging herself to the breakfast bar, she sat, jet-lagged, with her glass of juice. The *marañón* at the juice bar, also known as cashew apple, excited her more than Raphael. *Finding love is more important than exotic tropical fruit*, she told herself. Maybe her sisters were right. *I'm going to ask the sloth what's wrong with me.*

The clinic, two huts over, had six two-toed sloths and two three-toed sloths that slept tangled in branches inside a giant stilted A-frame. Joanne entered through a screen door into a mini-forest of furballs. She was only vaguely aware of their sluggish presence. She hoped Raphael wasn't there. A lady in khaki came in from another room to greet her.

"I'm Nancy," she said. "Head sloth nurse."

Joanne introduced herself and her agenda. Nancy took a step back at Joanne's boisterous demand to hold a sloth pronto.

"That might be tricky," Nancy whispered. "They sleep all day."

"What about the therapy?" Joanne asked. She pictured a sloth with a clipboard, taking notes while his patient, reclining on a couch, expressed his emotions.

"People pet the sloths to rejuvenate," Nancy said. "Come back at sunset."

A sloth clinic, Joanne realized, was badly suited to her impatient nature. She hated waiting around. Even in her sleep, Joanne was either on the way, or paused briefly to observe, annotate, and resume. Her dreams were as tidily packed as her suitcases. A dozen little stories in each dream, like balled pairs of socks, ready for Joanne to flip through and meld into jaunty magazine articles. Waiting around was wasting time. Wasting time implied letting life pass by without turning it into a story. What was she supposed to do all day while she waited for the sloths to wake up—seduce more strangers? What else was there for her to sum up?

Joanne killed time in the bromeliad garden, but being alone wasn't making her feel better. It was true: she did take up projects that guaranteed her a solo experience. She thought of Raphael again, and the stick bug. Trying to connect with people made Joanne feel marooned; why was that? Seated on a rock bench beneath a monstrous and majestic staghorn fern, she wished she had a travel companion. Not a stranger, but a person she had history with. A beautiful fern like this, then, would have been more momentous as an object of worship. She recalled feeling similarly in Alaska, wishing she had had a friend or lover there to share that moment when she first beheld a shark-sized carrot. That moment when the farmer stood the carrot up and it was as tall as her. Witnessing the world's wonders alone made Joanne increasingly doubt reality, and also undermined her belief that her writing could reflect these brushes with beauty accurately. Since no one was there for this reality check Joanne craved, she rebelled by conjuring up a clipboard-sporting sloth therapist.

"While I'm off researching and holding phone conference

calls," she told Doctor Sloth, "VV and Dena slug bottles of sake during a Samurai film fest, or dress up like ragamuffins to shakedown dancehall moves. I hate spoiling their fun, but they piss me off so badly."

The sloth was confused. "You obviously care about them," he said. "As you're talking to me."

"Mom worked herself to the bone for nothing," she said. "It isn't fair for my sisters to take an opposite, irresponsible tack."

She thought of their other most recent fights, over Joanne's refusal to taste test sophisticated tea blends or to get a makeover. She was constantly under deadline, never had time to make her sisters understand that somebody had to pay bills. Thus, they always came to an impasse; traveling was Joanne's only defense. While globetrotting she could remember her sisters more fondly, from afar, and felt in her gut how much her family meant to her. She hoped that loving them during crises—narrowly averted plane crashes or fantasy sloth conversations, for instance—psychically substituted for actually facing her irreconcilable relationships.

"Take up a social sport, like volleyball," said the sloth. "Something you can play with your sisters in crowded Brooklyn parks, where zillions of other people play those same sports, like sports zombies."

Okay. Joanne would commit to something as boring as volleyball for her sisters. VV and Dena were so revoltingly athletic.

After sunset, the sloth clinic was bustling. Or so Joanne would write in her article. Really, four kids in a hut hugged sloths while slung in cushiony white hammocks that looked like burritos. To reenter the hospital at dusk, Joanne had pulled rubber galoshes on over her sneakers, so as not to track mud in from other parts of the forest.

"Sloths are sensitive to bacteria," Nancy told her. Joanne wrote this down.

"Yes, but is there a sloth I can hold?" Joanne asked. It was her second day in Costa Rica, she was flying out the morning after next, and she hadn't even touched a sloth yet. She was really getting stressed.

"I'll check to see if any of the sloths feel like meeting someone new," Nancy said, wandering off into another room. She came back in. "Not yet," she said. "Why don't you have a look around?"

Who's healing who? Joanne wondered. But there comes a time when one has to be for humanity or against it. The sloths certainly weren't to blame. A magazine sent their writer down to bond with sloths, and no sloths were offered.

"*Pura vida*," Nancy called, sipping soda through a tall pink straw then holding it into the dank, tropical air.

"*Pura vida!*" everyone else said, toasting the sloths. Pure life. Everyone seemed to have a soda but Joanne.

Where's my damn sloth? Joanne wanted to scream. She pictured VV getting sloth attention without even having to ask. *The harder I try*, she thought, *the less I make things happen*. Joanne needed to get with the humans if she wanted any chance with the sloths at all.

The disconnect was unbearable. Joanne marched down a short corridor to see the only other room in the clinic. There were more hammocks, and four more people holding sloths. No one spoke. They were swinging and hugging their rented pets. The scene was infantile. Humans rocked in their burrito cradles, tucked under tan, fuzzy covers.

Joanne had nothing better to do than to watch. While at first she felt trapped in an exposed way, like a pinned beetle, she moved her shoulders in small circles, easing her tense muscles, then leaned against the wall, slipping her pen and steno pad into her pocket. She mentally noted the demure noise of hammocks swaying, and implored herself to write this down later, still unable to capitulate to the benign setting. Acquiescence was not in Joanne's vocabulary; she had never considered the idea that when one can't move, there are still ways out. Forced to sit with her feelings of captivity and helplessness, she managed to locate a certain comfort in her lack of options. Nothing was happening here. She had to get this piece done and she was safe in a hut, surrounded by sloths. She was not lost in the jungle being tracked by a jaguar. *What really*, she asked herself, *is so bad?* Her feeling of ensnarement shifted slightly to make room for a flash of controlled relaxation, as if Joanne was muffled in a womb. *Nothing* was okay. She could write about that nothing, later on, if she had to. Impatience was the snag, not the sloth torpor. This was her introduction to calm.

Nancy entered the room and handed Joanne a sloth. "Hold him tight," she said. "And don't rub his fur the wrong way."

This sloth was really friendly. He smiled at Joanne, as she noticed how his coat went backwards, up his arms instead of towards his fingers. She stroked his bristly, matted hair from his hand to his shoulder.

"That's his camouflage," said the nurse. "It makes him look like moss. Sloths actually grow moss in their coats. They're living ecosystems."

Joanne wanted to be an ecosystem. A couple weeks prior, VV and Dena had coerced Joanne into running nude, save for snow boots, while howling through a quiet neighborhood park during a Manhattan blizzard, and Joanne had been surprised at how much she liked it. They weren't arrested, and at least if it hadn't produced in her a sensation of placidity, it took her mind off of work. It had been too cold and too fast to think of deadlines, and Joanne never would have done it, or loved it, without her sisters.

The sloth hugged Joanne, and gave her a quick, dry lick on her neck.

"He likes you," Nancy said. "He'll sleep with you now, if you want."

Sleeping with a sloth, huh? Joanne thought. A burrito hammock awaited her. She felt awkward bedding down with a sloth on top of her, but couldn't wait to get to know this sloth better. He buried his eyes by leaning his head face down on her chest, then looked up for contact. Hoisting him over her shoulder like Santa's toy sack, she plopped down in the hammock and let the animal sprawl across her torso.

Joanne couldn't tell if the sloth was awake or asleep; he was in some in between state. Time grew prehistoric, reverting into a previous eon. These sloths were living in some type of minus time, exuding a rejuvenating lethargy. Joanne was not worried, right now, about her sisters or about tomorrow. The sloth expected nothing from her, and gave nothing in return, gave a great and beautiful kind of protracted nothing, one that Joanne wanted to wrap herself in like a fur coat. Swamped in sloth, Joanne inhaled and noticed he smelled like old piano and white cheddar popcorn.

JACKPOT (I)

We'd checked in to the hotel for a grand international gathering, and had each found on our beds silver lamé bikinis or speedos alongside big bottles of whiskey and tequila. Pillow mints were for rejects. The hotel was on a private beach where yachts coasted in and out of the inlet, and people wore clothing that implied nudity. The other ladies had packed entire suitcases of lingerie. I'd packed a mere pair per day.

Liquor bottles lined the jacuzzi's edge in the rooftop suite reserved for the birthday boy we were there to party with. I took shots whenever the jets switched on. In the far corner, two Euro boys groped each other to decide whose balls were softer.

"So soft!"

"No, yours are soft!"

I tuned out the balls, taking note of the men's lightheartedness instead. One guy floated over the other and made baby waves. I went with it. A sex bath is cool with me. In my corner, a skinny Swiss friend sold me on milk & oil baths. One quart of milk, a drizzle of olive oil, optional honey. *Definitely adding honey.* Apparently every Alpine boy grows up taking luxurious baths. No wonder their nuts are supple. I pictured him in lederhosen pouring buckets of milk over himself. His forearm was flocked with peach fuzz like a reindeer antler.

"Soft," I said, looking down into our shady tub. Everyone was naked. My pubes waffled underwater like a black seaweed patch. I twirled my new wedding ring, then lifted it out to make sure the chlorine wasn't discoloring its dainty gem. It was square to worry about it. These people have mass diamonds, right?

Swissy's boyfriend wandered over, unrobed, and climbed in. I got out, tied on some terrycloth, and headed downstairs to see my own soft new husband. This extravagant honeymoon was a gift from the birthday Godfather who was still in the hot tub.

On our room's balcony, Pandora was shoving ice cubes up her pussy. She was impersonating a slot machine, one where no man can hit the jackpot. I wiggled in for a good view while deep funk played. Four people huddling around a lady crotch-melting ice cubes might be criminal in silence or sleazy with techno. But funk was making the scene revolutionary. Zeus, wrapped toga-style in the crisp white top sheet he'd yanked off our bed, called Pandora's pussy an antique clock. I guessed he meant her body was timeless and beautiful, which it was.

"How Greek of you," I said to Zeus. He watched two more cubes disappear then passed out on our bed.

Hermes smoked a Capri cigarette in a monkey fur coat. He only wears exotic fur.

My new husband, wearing a shirt and no pants, sipped a glass of wine. He needed a nickname, fast.

"Pan, for no pants," I said, kissing his cheek. I was impressed he was hosting an impromptu mini-party.

Once the ice bucket was empty, Pandora twisted the cap off a bottle of JD and trickled it down her butt crack to make Crack on the Rocks. Zeus passing out mid-show had forced her to reinvent the act. I've known Pandora for fifteen years and she's always a wellspring of experiments.

"Where are we?" I asked Pan.

Our daily life is swell, but it's not this theatrical. He put his arm around me. In this alternate universe, Pandora was challenging someone to a competition. The bride? I just don't think about pussies that much. Pandora wins the trophy. I'm a space virgin who occasionally bumbles onto her orgiastic planet.

Pandora carves her initials into every place she visits. For instance, we met under a table. Many years back, I dropped a cigarette at a party, bent down, peered under the tablecloth, and there she was, shoegazing. Crawling under to join her, I asked her what she loved about foot apparel.

"Don't ever call it that," she said.

We shared a smoke and planned a Russ Meyer movie marathon. I was into boobs, I told her, since I like how the word in singular is a palindrome. I wasn't a threat to Pandora because she only dates women who look like James Dean. After the breast talk, she left our fort, tore a lampshade off a nearby lamp, and danced around the room with a shaded head, declaring Russ the king of busts. People love her or hate her.

The following morning, some of us ferried to the birthplace of twin gods Artemis and Apollo. On this unpopulated island, millennia-old bricks still walled in areas where people had worshipped the Goddess of the Hunt. I could smell the Artemis cult—wise women with gold bracelets coiled around their biceps, drizzling liquids on each other. These were women who kept panthers on leashes. It wasn't Lesbos, but it was as close to Wonder Woman as I may ever get. The island was a desolate, scorched place, and it was over a hundred degrees.

Our group separated and I strolled with Pan through a ruined city of crumbling columns, stairs, aqueducts, and statues. We stumbled upon a turquoise and mustard mosaic-tiled ballroom floor, patterned with fish swimming around a mermaid that had been danced upon two thousand years ago. I kept a cloth tied over my head, Muslim-like, to avoid sunstroke. After two hours of strolling, I verged on summer heat hallucinations. The mermaid oracle appeared to tell me now that I'd married, I could die a happy woman.

"Don't take me now," I pleaded with the heat vapors. "I finally have a husband to care for."

"This moment in your life is fleeting," the oracle declared. "Beware the future."

This oracle was beginning to sound suspiciously like myself, the saboteur. I evaporated her by telling Pan I needed a rest. Locating a cave—three slabs wedged like Stonehenge into the hillside—Pan helped me scramble uphill and squirted water on my face. We inhaled a package of soda crackers, and Pan asked what my problem was.

I was feeling too quiet to explain that the oracle was undermining my romantic moment. Crushing silence was my only weapon against sexier women who might try to usurp my treasured love, sexier women who were only sharing my honeymoon because Pan and I had rolled our honeymoon and this birthday celebration into one fat spliff. I'd always presumed myself above Pandora's lowbrow challenges. The atavistic female struggle was already kicking in. I was excited that I had a husband to defend, but I didn't want to pander to the woman who loosed evil on the world.

"Where were the lion fights?" I asked Pan, gazing down at an amphitheater. Downhill to the right stood a gargantuan foot left from a colossus who had been one of the world's seven ancient wonders. This was my idea of a turn-on: a cave with a view of a hand-carved stone foot. Forget spying designer shoes from under a table. I wanted to have sex right here, a million more times than I had wanted it after the Ice Capades. Pan and I were desert lions. The sheer age of this place made it sexier than a boutique hotel room.

"Lions!" Pan said, pointing down to a row of stone cats, silently roaring at the sun.

"They look alive," I said.

Back on flat ground, Pan showed me the case of painted glass eyes that had fallen out of the lion heads next to us. These were balls I could get into. Arranged in rows, they gave off mysterious airs. *If an island's history is deeper than mine*, I thought, *how can I leave an impression?* Centuries of tragedy and scandal had boiled down to a vitrine of painted marbles.

I spotted Pandora's shoes from across the field: bright yellow rubber open-toed heels with ankle straps. Her magenta hot pants were tacky. I recalled our wedding, where as our maid of honor Pandora came disguised as a karate black belt—there are more photographs of Pandora karate chopping guests than of Pan and I combined.

I consider my best friend a sister, which means I don't always like her. She's related to me because we share qualities. Pandora is my mirror; she shows me things I hate about myself. How would I know what to fix if she didn't go everywhere with me to point out my flaws? The night we met, of course, I questioned wanting a friend who dances around wearing a lampshade. When I said, *N-O*, I knew I needed her. I want to believe that one can never be too free, and that I just need more training. But too much free spirit can make those around you uptight, as they pick up the slack.

When I met Pan, Pandora and I were roommates and she was dating one of her James Dean girls. This one had a short ash brown pompadour, wore a leather jacket, and spoke a hushed Marilyn Monroe/Elvis dialect. Jimmy Four, I called her, never hung out much; she'd just come in and head straight into Pandora's bedroom. Daily, I could hear them doing it through the thin wall that separated our rooms. Since Pandora was a drummer she showed me all the drumsticks and maracas they used as dildos. I even got a demonstration of why this egg-shaped shaker was Pandora's favorite masturbation tool.

"It makes you feel like a mother bird," she said.

This was one of the few times I piped up and said, "Way too much information, dude."

"What, you don't jerk off?" Pandora asked.

"Well, yeah, but…"

"Go tie your apron on and bake some pies, prudie," Pandora said. Pie baking was our generic wholesome activity.

Pandora stuck out her tongue, marched into her bedroom, and slammed the door. She banged out Hendrix's "Foxy Lady" on her drum kit, then after a silence her and James started moaning and grunting. It was at this moment that I decided I wanted my own James, who wouldn't lurk around waiting to be poked with the drumsticks Pandora had just jammed out Classic Rock beats with.

At sunset, the beach was for the no-tan-line crowd. I wore a more substantial black bikini bottom because my ass looked like a Mylar balloon in the silver lamé. Some ladies were coffee colored—one Corsican woman had beautiful tan lines on her neck from where her long hair for years had covered her skin. I was splotchy bronze like hash browns. But I liked how my teeth glowed an especially attractive white compared to their usual tea-stained yellow.

Pan sipped tin cups of white wine from the taverna, and in between drinks he swam out for rock diving. I snorkeled away in the salty, curative sea. Underwater, green spiky anemones and purple crabs coated boulders. A spotted squid disappeared in a puff of sand as soon as I realized what it was. I imagined he had returned home—to a ruined Pandora statue, her heels stabbing the seafloor like prehistoric anchors colonized by seahorses. The seahorses' prehensile tails curled and uncurled as they navigated marble stilettos overgrown with burgundy sea plants. I love seahorses!

Pandora didn't flinch when I described this vision of her, ruined and swarmed with seahorses, back on the beach. She continued sipping her ouzo in silver lamé, a silk sunhat, and Chanel sunglasses. I plopped down next to her.

"You're all wet!" Pandora said, dipping her fingers in ouzo and flicking them at me.

"There's a giant underwater statue of you out there," I said.

"Where?" Pandora asked.

I pointed one cove over.

"Pan's still there," I lied. "We followed a squid to a sunken statue of you wearing stilettos and surrounded by seahorses."

"Stilettos?" Pandora asked, intrigued.

"Size fifties," I said.

"5-0," Pandora said in awe. "But seahorses?"

"What's wrong with seahorses?"

"Are they even animals?" she asked.

"They lay eggs," I said. "And the males carry and deliver the babies. Want to go see?"

"No," she said. "That's nasty."

Pandora's definition of nasty is often different from mine.

"Half the reason I traveled here was to see seahorses," I said.

For a second, I thought she was boring. I had the edge. As far as she knew, I had seen the seahorses. She was such a debutante, coming halfway around the world to sit around and drink. But then, I flew out to see seahorses, which is equally weird. Where was Pan, with his brilliant rationality, when I needed to sort this out? Or would he have refused to dig me out of the competitive pit I was lowering myself into?

I have a Seahorse bookshelf in my living room library. I guarantee Pandora has a Sex Toys section. She has her glamour, and I have mine—in my black suit, fins, mask, and snorkel, I looked like a marine biologist. That's seductive in my book. We love different things, but each a lot. Pandora worships her pussy, and I am vaguely devoted to things that symbolize a pussy—caves, pregnant seahorses. So maybe I'm too removed. At least I'm not a man-eater.

"Swim out there with me," I said.

Pandora finished her ouzo, set her hat and sunglasses down, and borrowed a mask.

There were no waves, only a sheet of transparent blue forming the horizon. Pandora's silver bikini was reflecting sunbeams off of it. It could have been a lighthouse beacon for lost boaters, but instead it attracted a school of metallic, shimmering orange guppies. To them, Pandora was the Mothership, the O.G.: Original Guppy. The school followed Pandora as we swam around the point, where I hoped there would be seahorses, preferably surrounding a sunken statue wearing high heels. Pandora reminded me of the mosaic mermaid.

"Look at the fish," I called, pointing down. Pandora put her mask on and looked at her feet.

"Those aren't guppies," Pandora said, coming back up. We looked again. The fish had pencil-tip-sized razor-sharp teeth. Pandora started kicking them away. We came up and ripped our masks off.

"They're man-eaters," I said, half-joking. "It's a new breed."

"Do they bite?" Pandora asked, drawing her legs up towards her stomach. She only asks me for information when she's scared, which proves she trusts me. The fish did look capable of gnawing us.

"They don't bite," I lied, staying a cool fifteen feet away.

Instead of paddling away, Pandora let her legs down and took her fins off, to test a nibble. I pulled my mask on and went under to watch. Though legs always look like things that attach to other things, they're peculiarly isolated. I watched this underwater man-eater documentary wishing Pan could see. The soundtrack was snorkel breathing. Pandora's undulating knees were the coral reef. Fish circled her calves, trying to nudge their lips onto her, with no luck. She said their teeth felt bristly, but weren't cutting. The guppies eventually took off, but the suspense was way better than seeing seahorses.

Pandora is 100% woman, and that's probably why she confuses me. Paddling there, watching her, I invented recipes for us. Pandora is part man-eater, part coral reef, part drumstick. I am part books, part caves, part marine biologist. I was glad I'd shared my honeymoon with her. Watching Pandora do tricks ultimately makes me love her more. Like the two men obsessed with balls, Pandora reaches out. Treading water, I knew I'd be a good wife if I could be half as brave as my girlfriend, even if she has stuck a wider diversity of objects up her crotch.

WORD SALAD

Chocolate Lily

I watch for wildflowers speeding through West Virginia. It's tulip-shaped on the map, so I stupidly assume the flower scene is heavy here. Instead of letting the landscape blur into green hilly strips, I focus my eyes on specific bloomers, following them the whole split second they're in my view. This is how I hunt flowers while driving. If something looks peculiar, I'll stop, reverse, and approach the plant to shoot a photo for later ID.

My first stop is to investigate what might be a *Fritillaria biflora* patch one hill over. Chocolate lilies look a lot like tulips, so it makes sense that they'd be here. I exit the highway, but the off-ramp concludes into a vast lake: nowhere to go except in. I plunge, my engine dies, and I crack my door to leap out of the big rig before it's submerged. I swim to shore and watch my vehicle sink into the blue lagoon. Refusing to drown in a truck. That's why, to me, flowers are nightmarish roughage, though trucks still arouse me.

Murderine

I'm a figurine representing a person about to get murdered, a cursed voodoo doll. A hand with red fingernails waves me around as a powerful talisman to worship and fondle. I'm an inanimate doll, not necessarily a woman, an animal, or a man, and that doesn't matter. What matters is that my dress flaunts an empire waist, and that my long, resplendent hair is braided.

Opal

With each sip of rose tea I take in this luxuriant bath, bubbles curl around my neck like a ruffled collar. The bubbles are lace, folding in and out into infinity like elegant costuming that transformed 16th century queens into birds of paradise. Tipping my mug back, I arch my eyebrows upwards pretending they're drawn on with grease pencil. In my mandarin collar with Dietrich brows, I also envision my lips over-painted past their lip lines with burgundy pencil. I wear, in this high tea bath, feather-toed slippers, a topaz brooch, a six-carat brilliant cut sapphire ring, and my golden hair is pin-curled up with opal barrettes. Fiery pink cabochons welded onto slender silver clips. My cat bats a half-dead mouse around the cat claw bathtub.

Boot Stomper

I'm the kind of snowflake who likes to be the last one clinging, crunchy and die-hard. I'm not delicate; my crystalline features are not the most quixotic, but at least I won't melt the second I hit earth. If I had feet, I'd kick tires to show how tough I can whack that rubber. Take me to the saloon and slip me into your drink. Flip my icy hair around like a whip. Pretend I'm a parrot and let me ride on your shoulder.

My snowflake pals are out of town and this village is a muddy mess.

"We're stuck in a mud bog," a woman says, wiping mud cakes off her boots. I'd clean her boots if I could; I'd frost them then melt, make her boot soles sparkle and shine. I watch her boots from the sidelines, hoping she'll stomp my curb next.

Shellevision

I live in a spiral conch, and I hate my name. It's too obvious—yeah, I live in a seashell. Living in shells on this beach to either side of me are fifteen other Shelleys who feel the same way. Why did all the shell dwellers who got pregnant in 1970 name their spawn Shelley? My mom must have been a member of the local Venus cult. On my one-inch mother-of-pearl shellevision, I watch crustaceous programming while administering elaborate manicures to my microscopic fingernails. This delicate box, powered by sample-perfume-vial-sized tube amps, has screened all the famous Shelley's, from Shelley Duvall to Shell Silverstein, who kids call Shelley. I admire watching these calciferous celebrities, but I'd rather perfect the application of teeny decals to my nails. Over three coats of high gloss enamel, for example, I prefer pinstripes to glitter dolphins.

Cruising: A Postcard Exchange

To: Looking for someone to love, You are so hot~!

From: OK I love you but you remind me of a skunk, or a spelunker. What. Are you a furry or…?

To: Yeah I wear animal costumes, so?

From: I just love skunks so much. Do you want to hook up?

To: Why do you assume that because we both like skunks we should have sex?

From: Well, yeah. What's your criteria? Skunks are specific I admit…

To: I just thought we should grab a salad bar together first, to develop a rapport.

From: I like nostalgia too. But what's the difference between skunks and a salad bar? Right?

To: There is a man crouched in front of my house, speaking Spanish into his walkie talkie. I will ask him.

The Phenomenology of Psychedelia

I ask for something and I definitely get something but I get something that I didn't expect.

Treehouses

Only because I, as a kid, got locked out of treehouses, am I the type of adult who snitches on secret treehouse builders.

The Albuquerque Savers

I flip through the most miraculous skirt rack I've ever seen in a thrift store. It starts with red skirts and ends on violet. To be exact, the aisle's left rack covers red through yellow-green, and its right rack begins with hunter green at the far end and arrives to me with purple. It is so exquisitely color-coordinated that I don't care about the clothes. I have the urge to walk slowly back and forth through this rainbow tunnel of textiles, huffing color. Lining the tops of the racks are extended rectangular shelves of baskets and purses, but wicker and pleather, today, don't hold my attention. The women next to me are hunting maternity pants.

Puppy Text

There are cute puppies, ugly puppies, aromatic puppies, puppies with dynamic hairstyles, puppies whose paws feel like flannel, puppies who are assholes and puppies who are as delightful as red velvet cupcakes. I am texting this story to you from my cell phone.

Jim's Rasta Vibe

Jim is a nickname for three longer names, each shorter than the last. *Jim* is *Jim-Ben* cut in half, which is a shortened version of *Jimjamin*, which is curtailed from Jim's full name, *Jimson Benjamin*. Jim to Jimson Benjamin is like Teddy Bear to Theodore Roosevelt, while Jimjamin sounds alluringly botanical, like Jimsonweed. Jimjamin belies Jim's Jamaican ancestry; Jimjamin sounds like *We be jammin'*. This is the story of Jim's Rasta Vibe.

We pull the car over on the two-lane mountain road, to an iron railing installed to prevent humans from falling into a rushing river at the bottom of this treacherous gorge. Jim steps out, pulls his t-shirt halfway off so it covers his head like an Egyptian pharaoh's headdress, walks over to the railing, and hops over. My job, for the rest of this jazz, will be to hunt the riverbanks for Jim's remains. Not fun, not cool, negativo.

Jim's cliff-jump is Rasta, because I suspect Jim will eddy out of the river to say, *I was only cliff-jumping, chill.* Jim is a producer of situations that come out of nowhere. My variable reaction is the erotic charge for him. Years ago, when we worked in the same office, he cornered me in the lunchroom.

"Want to do it in a bathroom stall?"

I didn't, but it was nice of him to ask. I like how he thinks. Why not make love on your lunch break?

Word Salad: a mixture of random words that, while arranged in phrases that appear to give them meaning, actually carry no significance.

HAIRPIN SCORPION

...ThE wOrDs lOOkeD LiKe tHiS As I sPoKe tHem. MoSt wOrDs sEEmEd bAcKwArDs, bUt iF I tYpEd tHat to yOu iT wOuLd bE tOo diFFiCuLt (T-L-U-C-I-F-F-I-D) tO rEaD. The words hung in the air like metallic smoke. We exhaled sneaky, silvery-scented, smoldering puffs. (Crack smoke has two qualities: the opacity to hide you from others and an eye-burning aroma to act as a distracting agent.) I smiled, watching a pot of mushroom tea boil on the hot plate. Everything was under control in our army tent, but it was about to get martial. We sat inside expecting desert winds to kick us around as the sandstorm twirled in its infant stage. The small rocks blazing in Zane's glass pipe were fear erasers. If I blew F-E-A-R in cursive letters into the air like smoke rings, like the airplane artist's love message in cloud writing, there would be the drug's valiant sword dueling with F-E-A-R then slaying it. Chunks of smoke would fall to the ground. I'm not always panicky, but when weather gets ominous I crawl into my foxhole.

Two strangers who looked like carnies—teeth blackened or missing, ripped Shakespearean peasant blouses—hunched in the corner of our tent taking hits off a nitrous tank. I wondered if Zane had packed the tank in his duffle bag, until I realized tanks don't fit in backpacks.

"Who are those guys?" I asked Zane.

"Yeah, huh. Get out of our tent!" he yelled. "And leave the tank!"

Zane was my ally. He was always himself, always in his body. Especially while high. He drove too fast and every time I rode in his Bronco, I knew I would die. He was 26, and I was 23. He played fast, noodly music exclusively on this road trip to Lake Mead in Nevada's salty desert. When I told him to slow down, he pointed to his radar detector.

"That's illegal," I said, lighting a joint.

"That it is," Zane said proudly.

Zane had stringy, curly red hair, and a speed-addict's rosy, pockmarked face. His cheekbones protruded out in a skeletal V. He was tall and the holey concert t-shirts he wore made him look even more like a bone man. I didn't find his punched-up but underfed look attractive. Rather, I studied Zane to learn how to live. I used drugs to gain access to his friendship, and to numb my instinctive sadness that he would die young. I felt gloomy picturing his demise, which I did constantly because deep down I'm a little goth. Knowing each day could be his last endeared me to him.

We became best friends one night after we bamboozled cash out of an ATM machine. Zane did it; I just spent the money. We drove into downtown Eureka, where we lived, to score. I still admire drug-dealer's code, the *I'm riding a bike*, or *wearing a blue shirt*, or *have new Nikes on* language that tells you who's selling. My friend Cara, who had just lost her baby in a car accident, was back at the house getting cranked. When we got home, and I saw her dull bleached hair draped over the coffee table littered with paraphernalia, I told Cara to leave; I never wanted to see her again. Somehow, a woman destroying her and her baby's life was more intolerable than a solo guy needling away his time. That night I thought, *No one here will learn their lesson.* But the following week, I still hopped into Zane's Nevada-bound Bronco.

Zane brought two dorks on our camping trip to Lake Mead, Micky and Beets. Beets—named after the root vegetable—was pudgy with a swollen purplish complexion, and he hobbled around like a gopher. Micky was taller and had hesher black hair covering his eyes, more death metal than speed metal. After arrival, and hitting the glass pipe in our heavy canvas tent, I took a beach chair to the edge of the lake and hallucinated flames spreading across its surface. The guys stayed inside the tent sucking nitrous.

I peeled off my clothes and set them in a pile next to the shore, then waded into the water after the flames died down. It was 90 degrees, black night except for the glowing lantern-lit tents. The water was tepid and glassy. Swimming out to the reeds, I listened to crickets chirrup. The reeds chirruped back.

One reed whispered, "Meet me."

Another reed said, "Do good deeds," and "Breeze," all these EEEs.

I put two and two together—EEEs, REED—Lake MEAD. I was really getting to know the place. I swam towards shore. Dripping, I walked to the beach to discover my clothes stolen. I wandered back, naked, into the testosterone tent.

"Where are your clothes?" Zane asked in a low nitrous warble.

"Pilfered," I said. I turned my bag upside down and poured out shirts and jeans. A three-inch-long translucent scorpion tumbled out.

"A scorpion is loose!" I yelled, yanking pants on.

"Stop tripping out," Zane said.

"Kiss this," I said, pointing to my rear as I dressed it.

"He won't hurt you," Micky said. He bent down and offered the arachnid some nitrous. The balloon blasted the small monster to the edge of the tent. The scorpion froze in the corner, probably from shock. I walked over to it, imagining the pitch a scorpion's voice would be high on nitrous, if it could speak—and noticed how the tip of its poison tail was shaped like a chive flower. Quite delicate, actually. Normally, if there's a spider in my space I'll scoop it up in a jar and set it free. But this was no spider. I let the scorpion be. Carefully shaking out each clothing article, I pulled on more wearables and exited, heading back towards my not-so-secret spot near the lake. I needed to escape this evil den of wicked, ugly scorpion lovers.

Zane and I were freshmen at the community college, although we hardly ever made it to class. We spent mornings on the bleachers watching the sunrise, trying to sip apple juice since we were too sick with drugs to eat. He was a fifth year freshman. *What are you doing with your life?* I'd think, looking at him. He liked cooking, even though he hardly ate and was lanky like a preteen boy. He was a talented chef, and spent rare nights cooking steaks for us on his dorm room hot plate. On this camping trip, there was no food along, not even gas station snacks. We'd even blown off buying alcohol. Zane was channeling his maniac this time. Why bother drinking when you have crack, LSD, weed, nitrous oxide, psilocybin, and speed?

I forgot to mention that Zane had pressured me into dosing before my lake swim; I hadn't wanted anything else in my system, but Zane called me a chicken so I set one small square on my tongue. The acid was kicking in along with the windstorm. Sand made gravelly grating sounds against the walls of the tent, which I watched bloat inward like sails on a ghost ship. Wooden poles barely holding the thing down rocked back and forth. There were no trees around, so I felt like we were all trapped in an hourglass. The sand gusts were noisy, like water torture. Soon I watched all the men filter out of the tent, covering their eyes with their arms and elbows to keep sand from stinging their faces. I sat on the lakeshore with a shirt around my head, watching them try to hold the tent poles in place. My pants and t-shirt were filling with sand; weighted, I was a human sandbag. I remained sitting, a hundred feet from the drama.

"Beets, grab the stake!" Zane yelled. His aura turned into a reverse shadow and glowed green as if his spirit would puke from getting nailed with sand pellets while being poisoned by Beets' idiotic presence.

Micky had both hands around one stake. Zane couldn't keep hold of his because whirls of sand were whipping him. The sand was a demon unleashed by the Shakespearean carnival freaks. Everyone was getting what they deserved. The night's catastrophe was falling into place. Lake water flamed up again. I stood up to get a better view, cupping my hands around my eyes like binoculars.

Zane yelled for me to come help. The tent was collapsing. I jogged over and tapped a stake in half-heartedly. I didn't want to interfere with the sand demon's wrath. Micky crawled inside the tent, now a jumbled pile of fabric, and emerged with a ball-peen hammer.

"Beets, hold that stake," Micky yelled.

"Don't hammer," I said. "It won't work." His hammer was ridiculous and so was he. Fate had the upper hand.

As Beets held the stake, Micky hammered, crushing Beets' finger to a bloody pulp. Beets was too loaded to pull his hand away after the first whack, and he got a good five more in before hunching over to hold his damaged finger in his good palm. Blood squirted out of the closed fist.

"Let me see," I said, prying his hand open. A flat, mushy appendage lay in a pool of dark liquid, its tip split wide open so the wound looked feminine, like a vagina. I expected it to start talking. *You should've...* it said in a whiny voice. I couldn't understand what the finger was saying I should've done. *Killed Zane?* I thought.

"Where's the sink?" Beets asked.

"There is no sink," I said. I was furious. What wrath had I incurred, sitting over there, watching water lap onto a lake beach? I took off my dusty t-shirt to wrap around Beets' finger, applying pressure the way I had learned in First Aid class.

"You need a doctor," I said. I felt semi-motherly because I was topless now, like a witch doctor.

"All I need is a bathroom," he said.

"There's a bathroom in town, Beets. I'll take you."

"No one's going to the emergency room at 4 a.m. high on acid, crack, and shrooms," Zane interrupted as he walked over from the other tent end.

"Are you the boss of smashed fingers?" I asked. "He'll bleed to death."

"No one's going to bleed to death," said Zane.

I kicked sand instead of Zane.

"Give me your keys," I said. Zane ignored me.

The shirt wrapping Beets' finger was gurgling with blood. Beets was pale and sweaty. Sand stuck to his forehead and his moist shirt, and it looked like he had a wasp hive on the end of his arm. Even though sand is porous, blood pooled on the surface of the sand at his feet. I worried he would die if I couldn't bamboozle Zane's car keys away. It was time to get crafty, but I began to cry.

Zane let go of the last dumb stake of the already collapsed tent and assessed the situation. Beets tried wandering off to a non-existent bathroom.

"Sit down, Beets," I said, grabbing his shoulder to still him. I faced the inevitable. "You're going to die."

"Don't TELL him that!" Zane said.

I entered the tent to locate a dry shirt to contain Beets' doomed finger. The scorpion seemed like years ago. Tomorrow, there would be a corpse buried in sand. I'd tell the police I didn't take him to the hospital, and they'd book me. The sandstorm calmed and I stopped shielding my eyes, even though I was already in the tent. Beets would bleed into first morning light, while I thought of ways to kill Zane.

Zane always exerted this false sense of authority. He had zero sexual grip on me, since he reminded me of a scraggly

Irish Setter. There was only life and death for Zane, though, and I liked this. He ignored everything in between. I knew what was running through Zane's head: Beets wasn't going to die, therefore he didn't care about the remaining plan. Appendages were inconsequential to Zane. He was nonplussed at parties unless people were diving off decks or having cardiac arrests in bathtubs.

I craved near-death adventure, until I got my fill with Zane. He was so gentle with me, weeks prior to this, the night we sat on his dorm room mattress for twelve-hours talking about how messed up life was. Gazing up at rock posters, Zane and I plotted against our healthy selves, destroying our bodies with real camaraderie. Zane almost died one night, and I got to watch his eyeballs pop out of his head while he laughed hyperactively. But recently, every time death neared, Zane denied its possibility, which made me suspect that he'd lost his edge.

I woke up in the reeds, far from camp. Sand was in my mouth, my hair, my eyes, and my ears. I never wanted to see those guys again. I was seven hundred miles from home with sixteen dollars in my pocket. I wandered to other campsites asking people for a lift, and found someone who was going back to California. I needed to gather my stuff, and slipped into camp to rummage through the disgusting pile of canvas that was once our tent. Hopefully Beets was still alive.

He was, but he was limply slouched in the tent mess, sitting cross-legged on the floor. I walked by without talking to him and leafed through our supplies, scattered in a fifty-foot radius. I found my wallet and searched it for a hairpin to hold my sandy bangs back. I grabbed my bag, feeling around for pins at the bottom. I got a warning pinch. Throwing the bag, that scorpion flew out, happy to have camped in its newfound tent, more stable than ours, happy to have weathered the storm. *Lucky thing*, I thought. I watched the scorpion curl its chive-stinger up to sting, as would my acerbic tongue should anyone speak to me. *Go ahead, Zane, try to feed me drugs one more time.* I hitchhiked home and never saw Zane again.

THE PERVERTED HOBO

Slidey was as slimy with green algae as ever. Bob, the husky, wished it were blue-green algae, the kind he once slurped off the rocky shores of an Alaskan glacial lake. Blue-green algae reminded him of wet rocks: slippery but spiritually clean. Nevertheless, Bob decided that Slidey was a sweet waterfall slide. Huskies aren't known to dwell on the past. This afternoon, Bob wasn't going to ruin it by getting wistful. He reared his head and gave a mighty howl.

Slidey was naturally worn-down granite. Bob loved hiking up to Slidey because he could frolic off-leash and there were no biting flies. He liked the blueberries and salmon that came in the Alaskan blue-green algae package, but again, for today he'd have to settle for a less pristine landscape. Mainland dogs don't get to travel to Alaska on a daily basis, Bob realized. He was lucky he'd been born and raised in Alaska before being shipped down to the desert, and that he'd had the opportunity to sire a sled-team's worth of pups that now rule the Iditarod. He'd heard about the sled race domination through the Husky Howl grapevine.

Bob met Slidey six years ago thanks to Bob's owner, Eugene Slidey, brother of the graffiti artist, Dougie Slidey, who had spent his teenage years tagging this stretch of creek back in the Sharpie Days. Slidey, smooth granite boulders + stream = waterfall, was named by Dougie who had written in wonky all-caps at the top of it, S.L.I.D.E.Y. The word was slanted down to the left, as if Dougie had passed out and slid down Slidey as he left his mark. The whole place, as a result, had a blasé slurred-speech feel.

Sometimes, interlopers slung ladies' panties on the branches lining Slidey's shore. Eugene didn't know if this implied that the mystery panty-slingers had conquered ladies there or if men had been wearing the ladies' underwear because some guys think they're more comfortable than tightey whiteys. He suspected men were at the bottom of it, as he couldn't picture women littering this scenic river. Granted, Eugene didn't have experience with women or their undergarments. Slidey verged on being washed up from the female lingerie situation.

The pink-orange sun hung low over Slidey as sunset commenced. Its white-yellow rays backlit the cottonwoods, while bees hummed soothingly in the tree canopy. *This golden hour is so ruff ruff*, Bob thought, meaning copasetic, panting as he trotted along the Slidey Trail behind Eugene, who had an aromatic sage bundle burning in one hand and a jug of water in the other. Eugene never went far without sage.

During their gentle upstream meandering, Bob noticed that, as usual, Eugene began to puff that mysterious, smelly white tube that meant his master probably forgot dog treats. *It would be astounding*, Bob sighed resentfully, *if Eugene would think to bring me some chicken strips on occasion.* Bob liked to dip these strips in the stream to let the poultry rehydrate. Dusk made Bob want to lick everything, chicken or not, including the speckled boulders they hopped. He paused to nibble dirt.

Eugene stopped and turned around. "Don't eat dirt, man."

Bob switched off, his nose now combing slimy granite for edible, second-rate algae. Bob wondered why Eugene called him a man. Bob huffed, licked the slime off of his long black clownish lips, winked at his owner coquettishly with his elegant eyelashes, and moved three feet over to lick more. Eugene gave up and continued hiking while his loyal white-gray husky hatched a plan. Bob would wait for Eugene to strip down to his cut-off denim swimming shorts at the top of the waterslide. Then he would fake-bark as if to run down to the bottom pool to greet Eugene, buying time at the top of the falls to mack pond scum. It wasn't Bob's fault he was starving because Eugene neglected to pack treats.

Thus unfolded another titillating afternoon. Once these two nonchalant fellows reached their destination, Eugene finished puffing his joint and tossed the roach into his favorite pool, a meditative but polluted portion of shore where foamy water ebbed in rings, dubbed by Eugene and Dougie the Watery Ashtray. Eugene thought the water was brown from high THC content, not from tannin leaching out of tree roots, common knowledge amongst non-stoned local riparian habitat naturalists. But Eugene wasn't about to whip out a science book.

"That water is so high!" he said, laughing to himself while his dog huffed the shore. Eugene had convinced himself over the years that the mystique of the unknown is best, having cultivated in his mind a homespun magic in which the web of life provided occult clues and signs to interpret mystically. Eugene measured his intelligence against how many nature clues he comprehended, but his friends and brother mocked this pseudo-shamanism. *Who are we to rate another's enlightenment?* Eugene wondered. He was one of many taggers who grew up in the Southwest, a place famous for its New Age tendencies. But equally famous there was Suicidal Tendencies, a lousy band that grown men still listen to when reminiscing over cases of beer about dropping acid in high school. Eugene straddled both worlds. He still sported bushy brown hair. It was unclear whether he was a total loser or if he was slated to be a priest. He suspected both; since he was one of the six gay men he knew in his small Arizona town, he practiced equanimity and had as much pride as he could.

While Eugene chugged water to squelch a coughing fit after his final intense inhale, a plush fifteen-foot-tall dog came walking on two legs from around the stream bend. *What the?* Eugene wondered. Bob barked and charged it immediately. The barks were idle warnings, though, nothing that scared the tall hairy beast. Upon this creature's approach, Eugene realized what was happening and loosened up. "It's cool, Bobby. He's human."

Bob stopped barking and wagged his tail.

"Hola!" Eugene hollered as the man neared. He only looked tall because he had several walking sticks tied to his back, laced with shredded leather and what appeared to be ladies' underwear.

Eugene noticed that dangling off this forest man's poles alongside myriad lacy panties were acorns, pinecones, and tiny green bows tied into clover-forms. Maybe this guy was a St. Patrick wannabe or an eccentric tree-lover, like Johnny Appleseed.

The man jingled a pole as if calling elves, proclaiming jovially, "Excellent sunset." He gazed up to behold its magnificence.

A real dipstick, thought Eugene.

"You're standing on Slidey," he said, smirking. He explained that Slidey was private with a locals-only tone. The dingleberry acorn man looked down at his decimated hiking boots planted right next to the cherished spot and chortled a hearty *Ho ho* just like Santa Claus. *Could it be?* Eugene wondered. That would kind of make sense, because it was only April, but Eugene had already wished for many things, well, mostly one thing repeatedly—a pair of chaps.

"Yes," the man said. "Slidey and I have had good times together."

"You know Slidey?" Eugene asked.

Bob, sensing Eugene's diminishing suspicion, started barking viciously in imitation of a Rottweiler he had seen on police reality T.V. Eugene grabbed his nose to subdue him.

"Slidey's family to me," the man said, tapping his pole to the ground like a rainstick.

"My brother made Slidey," Eugene said.

"No shit," said the man, extending a filthy hand to shake. "I'm Eugene."

"I'm Eugene too!" said Eugene. *Doppelganger?* He looked at the panties strewn over the other Eugene's poles and asked, "Are you behind the underwear deal?"

Old Eugene nodded. He reached back as if to unsheathe a sword, pulled a couple pairs of underwear off his sticks, and chucked them into a cattail patch. It was a confrontational slapstick move, too advanced for Eugene or Bob to comprehend. Part yahoo and part bliss. Who was this perverted hobo?

On the spot, Eugene was forced to remember, through his medicated pot haze, the day his mom came home fifteen years ago and announced his dad, Eugene Sr.'s, death. The conversation with his mom had faded over time but his rage remained. Eugene's hooligan boy life with his awesome renegade father had been prematurely terminated. His mom claimed that his dad had died in a river rafting accident, when the inflatable raft that he and five others rode the rapids in wrapped a rock and drowned them.

"Rocks don't kill people," Eugene told his mom in denial.

"Those damn rafts do," his mom said. Her coldness set reality up as something airy that could be popped at any moment.

He had trusted his mom in the past but when his dad died he began to see her as the family interloper. Eugene had always felt suspicious about losing his dad. There was never a wake, for example, just a jar of ashes, which could have been from any joe schmoe.

The day their dad's vase appeared on the dining room table, Eugene's little brother sat beside him in silence, early in the war between mom and son, waiting to see what Eugene would pull. Eugene chose retreat, so the boys retired to their bedroom stocked with two twin beds, *Playboys*, and candy. Eugene laid *Dark Side of the Moon* down on his turntable, put the headphones on, and dropped out. Dougie sat there on the edge of his skinny bed adorned with outer space bed sheets, slumped beneath a black light poster featuring the evil dwarves that haunt mushroom overdose victims, and waited for his brother to finish listening so he could mastermind their dual survival from here on out. Eugene stared at the sheets and wished he could transport to that corner of the universe they depicted. He had always preferred the company of men or space aliens to women, including his mother.

Who would teach them how to elk hunt or how to rescue trucks from the quicksand rampant in the nearby red rock river valley? They'd had big plans to become cowboys, albeit Eugene's vision, he'd assumed all along, was probably a variant on his dad's. Deep down, Eugene's cowboy vision included playing lasso with a buff cowboy who would hogtie and manhandle him. Now that those hopes were dashed, the boys vowed over pinpricked fingertips to be river haters.

"Rivers are lame," Eugene told Dougie, when the Pink Floyd record was over.

Eugene felt betrayed by Slidey, who had allowed another human to visit and bestow upon his shores gaudy accoutrements. Panty slinging was a cowboy move, Eugene decided, thinking back to the years he struggled to substitute his macho, muscle-obsessed homoerotic fantasies with a more benevolent, sage-smudging kind. This alleged other Eugene, as he set those panties free like a dandelion releases its downy seeds, conjured so many despicable emotions in Eugene that had gelled over the years into something like an allergy to cowboys. All that attraction and repulsion, including his old, supposedly cured hate for rivers and their murderous ways were packed into his reaction to the panties. Eugene was so offended by what he decided was a cowboy panty-slinging move that he was almost turned on by it. He pictured this very cowboy bending him over a river branch and…

Eugene stood facing Eugene. Bobby algae-grazed while Eugene's emotions went haywire. Eugene's face felt hot; he didn't know what would happen if he called the man on his fake cowboy-hippie attitude and dipstick-like qualities. He was a hater, in part, but not a fighter.

"I'm trying to feel peaceful right now, man, but it's really hard with your intrusive vibes," Eugene said to the white-dreaded wizard bejeweled with green bows and seedpods. Eugene himself had lustrous curly brown locks tamed by a bandana and was wearing a tie-dyed t-shirt and threadbare cargo shorts, but didn't want to admit that they shared a certain hobo style.

"What vibes, my son?" Eugene asked in a pious voice.

My son. Eugene had suspected for a few years following the tragedy that his dad had merely *escaped.* Gone away someplace real but intangibly distant, like Eugene's dreams. He couldn't send mail or call, but suspected his dad was doing all right somewhere far away. His dad never felt dead to him. He talked to his dad in dreams at least once a week. *Hey dad, why don't we have a smoke sometime? Do you date girls? Did you know I'm queer?* There was so much he yearned to tell his dad, not in his dreams or in a marijuana-induced hallucination, which is what this was if he was even allowing himself for one second to wonder if this was his father, his father's ghost, or Santa. But what the hell.

"Dad?" Eugene asked bluntly.

Eugene Sr. winked and tossed some more panties into Slidey's pool like a true forest faerie. Eugene's father wasn't dating girls either, it appeared, and Eugene gagged at the thought that he'd been aroused by… Bob wagged his tail and went up to Eugene Sr. for a grandpa chin scratch. The sun was setting now, and the trees turned black in silhouette against a periwinkle sky. They could see the Big Dipper. Outer space made its way into Eugene's life once again.

When you see a person who isn't definitely flesh, it's hard to end the moment because ending it means risking goodbye. Eugene was so moved that he didn't care if his dad was a ghost or if the Eugene-Sr.-rafting-death story was a farce. Eugene's mind roamed as the men sat still together on Slidey, letting night come. There were many ancestral appearances amongst the region's Native Americans, and supposedly lots of apparitions in general. He had always wished ancestors would visit him—thus the sage obsession—but this was the first time. His dad was the kind of person who would've disappeared because he had always been an undeniable recluse. Eugene wanted to embrace his father but was too scared that if he were a ghost, Eugene would hug air and their visit would end in a cloud poof.

Bob, unhindered by such lofty thoughts, sauntered up to Eugene Sr. and nudged him to let the men know that it was getting too dark to see and that they should all go back home for a celebratory chicken dinner. Eugene Sr. did not evaporate, and his son realized that indeed, his father had left him for a solitary life in the woodlands. Instead of feeling resentment or abandonment, Eugene couldn't believe his good luck at having a live dad again.

"Do you eat chicken?" Eugene asked his dad.

"Does Slidey have algae?" his dad answered, meaning obviously yes, to which Bob licked his chops, and the men headed home.

But chicken dinners don't last forever. The men and their dog roasted and devoured two chickens, savoring each rosemary-infused bite and gazing at each other fondly as though the meat represented their bodies and by finishing the meal they'd lose contact. Eugene had never understood the notion of transmogrification—that by eating a symbolic food one is actually consuming the worshipped one—but now he did. The chicken tasted as good as having his dad back.

Eugene Sr. said, "You look good, son. I like your hairdo."

Eugene looked at his dad's white, tangled mop and couldn't say the same. "You look like a hobo. So, where have you been?" he asked.

"Hoboes are cleaner cut," Eugene Sr. said. "And they don't toss panties. More on that later. Call Mother and Dougie to tell them I'm alive. I'll tell you all the story at the same time."

Eugene entered the living room and pretended to call, but secretly talked to dial tone. Dougie was off who knows where with his trailer trash girlfriend and Eugene hadn't talked to his mom in ages. He didn't want to have to explain everything. She wouldn't be able to just get in the car and come; she'd have to hear the whole story first, have a close-call heart attack, and then call a friend to gossip. Spontaneity was not in her vocabulary. She'd been anti-adventure since her husband's presumed death. Eugene wasn't ready to share his dad, anyway. This was the manly attention he'd craved for over a decade, and had never found in boyfriends. It was so much better than sex. *Why am I thinking of sex? Who is the real pervert?* Eugene was jolted by this mental disturbance, but wedged it carefully in the back of his brain so he could dwell on adoration.

"They're on their way," Eugene lied, returning to the dining room. Bob, picking chicken bones clean under the dining room table, knew a lie when he heard one and nudged Eugene's leg in alliance. He wasn't thrilled when he had to leave his sweet litter of husky pups in Alaska, but he wasn't into revenge and had no plans to spoil Eugene's father-son reunion.

"That's a sensitive dog you have there," Eugene Sr. said. "He's keeping secrets for you." Bob, who had made eye contact with Eugene Sr. as he spoke, turned quickly away.

"Bob taught me how to love," Eugene said, reaching down to stroke Bob's voluptuous back. "I hated all forms of life after I thought the river had gobbled you up."

"Rivers don't kill," his dad said. "It was the rock that cut me, bad. I floated downstream all the way to Ciudad Juárez, unable to land because coyotes, attracted to my bleeding wounds, stalked me on shore. I will never swim again. I am now a terrestrial man."

"I see you like acorns," Eugene said, thinking of a tree's grounding, rooted nature. "How did you find Slidey?"

"I smelled the marijuana," his dad said. "What are you doing out there, getting high all the time and sliding around like you have nothing better to do?"

Eugene saw nothing wrong with a middle-aged man partying on a rockslide.

"I could ask you the same thing," Eugene said. Dinner was barely over, and his dad was already critiquing him. *If that's how it's going to be*, Eugene thought.

"Dad, why didn't you tell us you were living in some cave watching us smoke reefer like a dang DEA agent?"

He'd been right; he did have spies for parents.

It had been so long that Eugene only remembered his dad—noble hero—as the parent he most resembled. Sometimes when he'd lie on Slidey's shores, he'd think back to when his dad was alive and try to recall his dad's face or laugh. During those moments, petting Bob, who was always at Eugene's side, helped jog Eugene's memory. Bob was his guardian now as his dad had been then. Bob, although he mostly was Eugene's chicken-obsessed canine son, also had fatherly qualities. Eugene would never admit, even to his closest buddies or his burly bear ex, Earl, how he thought of his dog as a dad. Bob's inquisitive nature, and the way his nose combed scents traveling through air like a peregrine falcon, reminded Eugene of his dad's radical abilities to locate missing objects. Eugene used to pan for gold with his dad, and they'd buried and unearthed in the yard several corked bottles of gold flakes as their own small lode. That way, they had wealth in case of apocalypse.

This extrasensory perception also translated into his dad's uncanny knack for detecting his son's fib.

"You didn't call Mom or Dougie, did you?" he asked, as they put cleaned dinner plates away and settled into rum and coke on the couch. Bob was curled up in the armchair, with his chin resting on the arm as he fell into a food coma.

"Mom will have a coronary," Eugene said.

"Have you ever taken her to Slidey?" Eugene Sr. asked. "I've never once seen her there."

"She's potamophobic," Eugene said. "Won't go near a river."

"What I'm wondering is," Eugene Sr. asked, "how you love the river after thinking I died in it?"

"Don't turn this around yet," Eugene said. "My questions first."

Eugene Sr. confessed shame about causing strife in his wife's life, and asked his son to help rectify it before he retreated back into the woods. It was too bad, he said, that Dougie had missed all the action, but it was Eugene and their mother that he had ventured back into the known world to make amends with. Eugene Sr. was a bit like a hobo, his son came to realize, in that he felt more connected to that land than he did with the wife and kids he left. Eugene didn't know what Dad's tramping life had entailed, other than upsetting his mom and nurturing his son's cowboy fetish. On the other hand, Eugene could now say he was plain chivalric compared to his dad, the family flake. With a burst of bravado, he told his dad his story.

"I hated rivers and all life within them," Eugene said.

His dad poured another round.

"I hated trout, frogs, and all the smelly aquatic plants. Dougie and I lost seven years defacing rivers and killing their stuff. I trapped so many river animals that Dougie said I could go into business selling pelts. Hell no, I told Dougie, I won't even feed my dog the fish out that forsaken river."

Bob's ears perked up, until his food coma recommenced.

"Over time," Eugene continued, "I softened. We were out there tagging that river almost daily, usually during sunset. One afternoon, when Dougie christened Slidey with a name, it dawned on me that we spent all our time on the river not because we hated it, but because it was our best friend and last connection to you."

With this, the men clinked their cocktails together and embraced.

After this heartwarming confession, Eugene desired to test his manhood again by taking the opportunity to reintroduce his parents. His parents had loved each other but never got along that well. Eugene's mom had been notoriously paranoid about his dad's bold expeditions. She claimed that teaching the kids self-sufficiency encouraged their wild streak, which probably was true. Their dad was known to take them out into the dunes, and leave them there with a compass and two water jugs. Their lives were often at risk. But why would a parent oppress a child's eager disposition? His dad's tough love had been evident to Eugene before the disappearance.

Eugene reached over to the armchair and rubbed Bob's head. He didn't attempt to shelter Bob from life-threatening adventures. When he found Bob in the animal shelter, and heard how he'd been mushed in no snow all the way down the continent, starved, pulling a packed sled, Eugene knew that in Bob he'd have a resilient companion. He wished Bob was capable of doing this kind of familial dirty work—mediating—the emotional junk a father would do for his son. *The ability to pull this off*, Eugene thought, *is what separates dogs from humans.*

Meanwhile, Slidey was flowing big time. It was April, and the snowmelt made the water rush vigorously, as if the tributary were racing to reach its destination—the majestic Colorado—before the sun siphoned it all into the sky. This is a region of dried up action. Things happen incrementally. The best thing about Slidey is that even when no humans are around, the waterslide gushes forth. Slidey has its own seasonal river dramas. Just because two guys gave Slidey a dumb name and a sacred purpose, Slidey is really just another river stone diverting snowmelt. As life changes daily, it's Slidey's job to learn and adjust with resourceful zeal.

Eugene didn't remember his mother's phone number. He had to dig into his backpack lined with sage and marijuana shake to locate his cell phone and then to scroll for his mom's name: Ismelda. His heart started palpitating as he looked at the call button. *Can dogs make phone calls?* he wondered.

"Press the button, son," his dad said. "Your mother won't cure my desire to use panties as trailmarkers, but it will be good to see her."

Do it for Slidey, Eugene told himself, thinking how pleasant it would be to never again see ladies' underwear.

"Trailmarkers, right," Eugene said.

His dad smiled and did a booty dance that belied silky material beneath his grungy canvas army pants.

Eugene wondered if he would have ever met his dad again if he hadn't allowed Slidey to permeate his psyche with nature's goodness. Slidey: the spot where Eugene's new life commenced for the second time. Bob, sensing Eugene's reluctance to dial, wondered if the phone was something fun to lick.

BABY GEISHA

The parking-violations officer bangs on the steamed up window before slapping a ticket under our windshield wiper. I have my head in Grizzly's lap, sitting in the driver's seat with his pants unzipped. His penis smells like a butter cookie. His hair, too, is long and butter colored. He is one of the greatest guys I know, only a friend. How did I end up here? He cracks his window and here's the game: he talks to the parking lady while I shut the world out and suck. *Don't Break My Rhythm. Don't Break My Rhythm.* The violations officer has cracked fuschia lip liner, unattractive in light of the job I am currently undertaking, and her blouse gives her the ruffled look of an ostrich.

"We're sitting right here, lady!" Grizz yells, tapping the window with his finger. His hard-on gets huge after he shouts.

She snarls a retort, the voice of a sex-starved woman. Ticketing people is the closest she comes to the thrill of getting a driver's seat blowjob.

I am neither an unfaithful wife nor a hooker. *What am I?* I feel old wondering this. I am neutral, still a woman who aims to please. Tapping into my nasty girl. Someone could host a talk show about this compulsion. A chain gang of middle-aged women stomps out on stage looking whorish with tussled hair. We all look like the ostrich meter maid, rugged. We went haywire after dry spells. *I suck dicks when and wherever*, says the lady with no bra, showing off a gap between her two front teeth. *I don't suck many but I relish the same few repeatedly*, the sultry librarian says. The audience looks to me, but I don't know what distinguishes me from anyone, including Lucy, the primitive cave woman who probably enjoyed this satisfying sexual act in caves with her hirsute male peers.

Another hardcore penis dream! These started over a year ago, when I began to think more about babies. I struggle to arise from this Ambien-induced slumber. This one ranks up there in oddity with my husband's notorious Ambien hallucination, in which he was flown on airborne serapes into the opened top point of a pyramid. It's already hazy, but what I take from my dream as I wake up is: I will never touch Grizzly, and Don't Break My Rhythm. My trusty motto. I dress down my repulsion with a straight girl outfit—jeans and a t-shirt—and drag myself into the kitchen for coffee.

My loyal husband prepares toast, awaiting news from the Dream Time. I feel conflicted about confessing I repeatedly dream about Grizzly's sexual organ, because in life I'm not even attracted to most men. But there's no point in lying because Taylor can read my mind. The next time Taylor and I do it, and I vigorously employ a new technique practiced in my subconscious, with someone else, he'll suspect something. But it's a free country, dreaming. There's no such thing as cheating in your sleep. I explain my dream over breakfast.

"Do you want to date other people?" Taylor asks, taking it as an insult to his own cock.

"That has nothing to do with it," I say. "It doesn't even have to do with men."

"So, Claire, do you want to do it right now?" Taylor asks, smiling wryly, still thinking it is about men.

I like his suggestion, even if that means we drop what it does have to do with. I love my husband tremendously, and morning sex is the best. If it weren't for morning sex I may stay dreaming all day.

It has been a month since we stopped living together. Today, I wake up alone in my rented room at a girlfriend's house. I live with her and her kid. Now I arise daily to a little guy playing pirate. "Hang in there, sister!" my girlfriend tells me on the roughest days.

I can't email Taylor, because I started fantasizing about checking his messages to eavesdrop, which I'm totally against. If he's off in search of a girl who doesn't want babies, imagining their flirt letters makes it worse. If I don't get an email from Taylor soon, I'll know he finally hates me. I cry for thirty minutes over half a box of tissues, try to get up, pull yesterday's clothes on, brush my teeth. These tasks seem vague and pointless. I pry the curtains open and feel burned, like a vampire. I'm hideous, missing the man who used to ask me about my dreams, which, even though they often include other people, are still ultimately about him.

Today, I realize more than ever my deep connection with beasts. I was never ruled by reproduction as a means to procreate, animal-like. Now that my body is telling me that it is time to bear a child, I feel unsafe making love, as if my inner-motivation is potent enough to will myself pregnant. It doesn't matter because Taylor won't touch me. He's in Hawaii now, surfing amongst those surf babes who don't demand anything of him but a co-ride on the next good wave. My feelings remain, so I'm left with my dreams and zero motivation to attempt meeting new guys who may not find me so abominable.

I know why I have these dreams: blowjobs are foolproof. Open wide. The virgin birth, in which Mary supposedly conceived baby Jesus with no male partnership, is a baby fever fantasy. The virgin birth is like a horror movie to me. Some of my girlfriends over the years, the ones Taylor and I least expected to become mothers, were suddenly hit with baby fever, and bam. There they were, standing big-bellied beside the men they'd found to father their children. Better than virgin births, and such cute babies. But still, I wish I could have a baby with the man I dedicated my life to.

To Taylor, sex is strictly a performance in which the more eloquently expressed the person's desires are, the better the results. It's theater, full of costume. Ideally, sex is his safe spot, where judgment is suspended so we can be free to try new things. *Taylor deserves someone experimental and brave*, I tell myself while he's out having fun, without me.

Last winter, I tried hard to change my predictably female ways. I had a crush on our friend, Rita, because she believes that thinking things through is the most backwards way to live. She acts purely on instinct. For example, one blustery day—five months ago now—the sun made a rare hot appearance in our temporary high-elevation mountain town. Rita was staying with us for two weeks. Our log cabin looked good, buried in snowdrifts, but I felt cooped up. Rita and I dropped everything, put our bikinis on, laid beach towels on the living room floor under a rainbow umbrella, and made spritzy soda drinks to have a beach party. We eventually got too hot to leave our bikinis on. It was the first day Taylor saw us lying together nude. "Cute," he said, heading out for a walk. I trusted that he meant that.

A week later, light snow fell through sunshine. Storm clouds rolled across a blue sky and the flurries generated these perfectly star-shaped snow crystals. I finished snowflake hunting in the backyard with my magnifying glass, velvet, and camera, and came in to prepare a pot of Nepalese chai, Rita's favorite. I took it into her guest room, to show her my snowflake photos. She had hung a pair of underwear, with the crotch burned out, on the wall.

Rita was painting blood drips down her chin. We'd been practicing werewolf make-up, and she was nailing it this time. She already had newly-dyed black hair, and was planning a photo shoot. We took a coffee break, and I couldn't resist her looking so bloody.

"Geisha, will you give me a massage?" she asked.

I put my mug down and gave her a shoulder rub, then did the rest of her back. I envisioned myself in white face powder, pale enough to pick up other people's colors, chameleon-like. I know real geishas are far from promiscuous, that they are skilled entertainers, but for this I embraced the prostitute geisha cliché. I owned the caricature; I needed that license.

"I feel like a businessman," Rita said.

"Yes master," I said, bowing.

Thirty minutes later, we were both naked and massaging each other over giant almond oil stains on Rita's bed sheets. Making Rita come made me proud. Rita is a sexpot who doesn't get emotionally hung-up, so I felt at ease that we could resume our friendship. I'd loved up my sister, family-style, and I was glad we had shared that. I love Rita and still do, and I thought Taylor would have been impressed. There was no competition. Not wanting my husband to feel left out, I gave him full geisha service directly after Rita's, one room over. The balance was restored, or so I thought. I was a pimp. I put Snoop Dogg on and felt like a bad ass. I dressed like a man for the next few days because my macho levels were through the roof.

"You did what?" Taylor asked, after asking why my new look was Gangster. Taylor stirred the bean stew with maniacal strength. His reaction was a surprise. He'd done the same a few times, with guys. Rita was in her room, listening to John Cage before she flew out the next day. I'd already resolved this with her, agreeing to keep it tamer from now on. She didn't want to be a girlfriend casualty, and I agreed completely.

"I slept with Rita," I said. "I'm trying to not be shy anymore. Do what I want, like you said."

"Don't pin this on me," Taylor said, looking away. Minutes

passed while we watched the stew boil. "Are you in love with her?

"I love you both," I said. "Why do I have to choose? I have too much love to give. It's overflowing. I always end up loving you. Don't break my rhythm."

"Too much love," Taylor said, marching out onto the cabin's porch. I followed him out.

"I hope this is temporary," he said.

"I don't understand why," I said. "You've always wanted me to figure out what I wanted in sex and do it."

"Do what you need to do," he said, heading back in. Each time in the past when he came back to me after being with guys, I'd felt that those were our greatest reunions. Maybe this time there would be no reunion and Taylor's double standard would rear its ugly head.

That geisha role cracked me open. I meant her to be sheer sexual exploration. I meant her to improve my understanding of intimacy. But once I unleashed her love, I sensed it bundled up and denied, laying dormant in my body like a hibernating bear. I've loved everyone too much since then. My geisha is not devoted exclusively to one person. She is an artisan skilled at pleasing others, who longs for a family. She is even more than pimp love. The geisha's love, I realized, is motherly. The geisha wants a baby.

When I met Taylor, I knew I loved him because I saw us growing old together. Those unknown life stages that would unfold between us came to me compressed, in Taylor, as a lodestone. To Taylor, sex never equaled babies. I was fine with that. I assumed since I'd met the right person that we could face the kid issue, in the future. That future is now.

Last week I talked to Rita on the phone about this urgent future that has pounced upon me like a predatory animal.

"Welcome to your biological clock," Rita said.

"I don't want to think about any of this," I said. "But I had this core realization that sex makes babies and that I have this magical power. Making love is something more instinctual now."

Talking to her about this wasn't awkward, despite our geisha day. I already miss her and like talking to her whenever I can.

"Its uncertain outcome is its main source of attraction," Rita said. She talks like a fortune-teller. "You're preparing for the uncertainty of the independent soul you'll give birth to."

As if the birth is already fated. Fate, the set motion, versus the uncertainty of controlling who we create. Rita is so insightful—I remembered why I love her.

"I can't stand this sadness," I said. "I'm afraid of sex now because the ritual is charged. It can't be a simple pleasure anymore. I hate that my body is telling me to do something I don't want to do—to think about myself and what I'm capable of producing. Sex is more selfish now. Am I still the geisha?"

"You're a baby geisha," Rita said.

Where will I land? Too much mystery, this sinking ship.

Then, there's Natalie. Natalie has been like a sister to me for twelve years, she's a powerfully maternal figure with an excess of love to share. She always wanted kids. She loves menstruation and kept a jar of bloody rags to soak in our bathroom when we were roommates. This was part good luck charm and part environmental effort. At that time, it was all I could do not to ask why my mother had kids with a man who couldn't commit to a family. I had stepparents, too, who struggled to muster up kid joy. Shaking off depressed parents encouraged me to discover nature's ecstatic life cycle. Watching vines crawl towards sunlight up tree trunks, or observing chipmunks growing from inch-long pink squirmy things into pert, striped rodents. Imagining ancient redwoods surviving the centuries. Birth was not necessarily a curse. Growth could be a positive experience. I tattooed the chipmunks on my inner wrist to symbolize my Fear of Babies cure, though I hadn't set my mind in any concrete way on one day having my own.

Six weeks ago, between when Rita left and I moved in with my girlfriend who has the pirate kid, Natalie and I took a road trip across the Southwest. She had no trouble understanding that I like both Rita and Taylor. She's not one to shy away; she digs deep into some female things that still make me squeamish, like vaginal mucus. Mucus: the worst word ever. For years before this road trip, she lectured me for not checking mine and keeping charts of how it looks and smells.

"Stop it!" I yelled over the phone. "That's disgusting!"

"Since when is your body disgusting?" Natalie asks.

You can't argue with women like this.

Now, she is thirty-three and announcing the good news on our drive.

"It's not that the rhythm method stopped working," Natalie said from behind the wheel. "I just let go, so nature could come."

I thought of another girlfriend back east, home raising chicks to practice childrearing. She's charting her months too. I recently enjoyed learning about ovulation from her, a process that I previously thought as alchemically mysterious as transforming shit into gold.

"I can't believe the rhythm method worked until now," I said. "I thought for sure you would have got pregnant years ago."

Natalie explained the elaborate fertility calendar she keeps, how she knows to the hour when she's ovulating and ready to conceive. *Women are not geese*, I think. *But we make eggs.*

"Ovulation is as cryptic as the Mayan calendar," I said. "Thank god for the pill."

"So, when are you having one?" Natalie asked.

My head rested sideways on the seatbelt strapped across my chest. The flat-topped, tan mesas speeding by out the window looked like baby heartbeats on an electrocardiogram.

"My life is not set up for that," I said, feeling a little dead.

"Taylor doesn't want one." Those sandy, eroded hills can't control having their tops lopped off by weather. I am not as powerless as a mesa, but I was acting like it. Just like the people who enliven the desert's desolation, like the Navajo who herd sheep on dry land, I am full of life. This road trip was what gave me the guts to tell Taylor I'd like a kid. It won't go well. It will be a stalemate. I didn't say any of this aloud, but Natalie knew. All my loved ones are psychic.

"You can do it, mama," she said.

We arrived to the Painted Desert, where pastel rainbows stripe the sandstone. We pulled off the highway into the park, and drove along the two-lane road that shows off canyons marring the vast expanse. To ignore certain desires would be ridiculous, like putting lotion on one arm at the expense of your torso and legs. My neglected layers aren't dissolving; they're just drying up. Where's my wisdom? Why won't Taylor have a kid with me? Why can't I have girlfriends? I pictured my torso shriveled into a raisin.

A long time ago, I got a second tattoo: a rainbow over my belly button. The tattoo artist warned me that the rainbow would stretch way out when I got pregnant, swelling like an image on a blown-up balloon. I saw the bigger rainbow in my future as a bonus. I should have been brave enough when I met Taylor to admit that maybe I'd like a baby in the future, even if he didn't want to hear it.

In the Painted Desert, I decided it was time for me to take up praying. I don't know how to pray and never knew what to pray to. But I obviously haven't been listening to my body. There are pieces of me that demand excavation. Newness, a kind of birth, often comes from nothing new: that which is returned and reclaimed.

"Pull a *Wicker Man*," Natalie said as we passed some petroglyphs. "*Take the flame inside you, burn and burn below, fire seed and fire feed, to make the baby grow…*" she sang with an Irish accent. She has the film's soundtrack memorized and this was not the first time she sang the song that scores the scene when women jump over a bonfire to bring fertility to their pagan village.

"Spring's here," I said to Natalie, alluding to *The Wicker Man*'s older meaning. Bright green sprouts budded on the cottonwoods in a nearby wash. I thought of geishas, twirling parasols under cherry blossom trees to honor winter's end.

"We need more ceremony in our lives," I said to Natalie. That's what I want: rituals and a family to practice them with.

The emerging leaves matched the pale, green sandy striation beneath the pink, orange, and yellow bands crossing the mesa like bars on sheet music. *This land is a symphony*, I thought. *Its composition is small compared to challenges I am about to face.* Will I listen to them all or will I let them fly by silently out the car window, as untranslatable vistas?

ESCAPE MUSHROOM STYLE

The animal hospital looked out upon the Wonder Wheel, an antique ferris wheel constructed of enough metal to build four skyscrapers. Plate glass windows in the waiting room gave the office, where Scruffles and I awaited a meeting with a soft tissue surgeon, a sleek feel. But carnival views don't make cancer fun. I stroked Scruffles, panting at my side with a golf-ball-sized tumor hanging off his dong. Snake-skinned ladies, men with gorilla wives, fire-breathers, poodles riding tricycles, elephantitis—it had all gone down here on Coney Island. Penis tumors were probably old hat. Made sense that a polluted beach would be a mutant culture hub. The world's oldest roller coaster loomed three blocks away. Was this vet going to be Siamese twins? Suddenly, it was moronic instead of ironic that I had considered administering dog cancer treatment at a facility bordering a decrepit amusement park. It was more moronic that I lived nearby.

"Scruffles?" I asked, scratching his woolly, red left ear. "Will you feel like a freak if we operate?"

Scruffles wagged his tail. Any question involving upped intonation at the end of the phrase produces in him a hope for fish.

I kept this appointment because I needed a surgeon's opinion.

The receptionist called us in. The doctor was not a Siamese twin but rather an emaciated man whose head reminded me of a *calavera de azúcar*, a Day of the Dead sugar skull. He groped my dog in a twitchy way and recommended something horrible.

"I'm not removing anything except the tumor," I vowed, petting Scruffles as I committed to keeping his body intact.

"He'll die," the surgeon said. Who was he to issue the death sentence?

I slammed the office door on the way out.

Soft tissue surgeons are too fixated on slicing to know what you do and don't cut. It's just not right. *Amputating a dog's penis is ludicrous*, I fumed in the taxi home. Scruffs panted, which I took as agreement. *What would I tell people when they ask where my dog's organ went?*

A week later, I left Scruff at home with three chew toys and took the train instead to ride the Wonder Wheel, whose cars, every quarter rotation, swing out on railings to the edge of the wheel's circumference. These cages, called the Danglers, dangle you over the boardwalk like a hooked worm being lowered into a lake of big mouth bass. My brother and I, swinging every two minutes, questioned how long our corroded cage would hold. We needed a meaningful conversation during our limited time together, while he visited. Today, we cried a lot. Privacy was nonexistent in this city, and we needed some. At least on the Wonder Wheel we had a car to ourselves.

"We're breaking up," he said, of him and his girlfriend. Tears welled.

"Don't amputate," I said, meaning, don't cut her out of your life. "It's not an ending, just a change."

Breakups or terminal illness, what's worse? Why compare? This was our discussion as our car teetered above skeeball players and kids ramming bumper cars. The toxic Atlantic was on the left, and the veterinary hospital lurked right. From up here, New York was semi-manageable, as microscopic as the toadstool world I prefer to live in.

"That's where they told me Scruffles had four weeks to live,"

I pointed down at the speck of an animal hospital, starting to cry. Wind whisked away my tears.

"That's some pathetic, salty rain," I said of my tears melodramatically falling on people below.

"Forget that vet," Lolly said. I nicknamed him Lolly when we were kids, because he had a big head on a skinny body, like a lollipop. "Scruff's a survivor."

"You'll live too," I said.

"Have you tried natural remedies?" Lolly asked. We gripped the bars sealing our metal cage and swung.

"Next week I take Scruffles to the herbalist," I said.

I have over a thousand mushroom photos under my belt. Last time I counted I was nearing four digits, so I began excursions to Rip Van Winkle's home turf, the clove where Irving's character allegedly fell asleep. Downy purple *Cortinarius*, a favorite fungus, grows under hemlock between blue slate outcroppings there. I may be approaching twelve hundred shots. I take road trips to my hideaway hills upstate after heavy rains. I've collaged my images, written amateur essays, and attended lectures at natural history museums about how genetic mushroom identification is outmoding Linnean taxonomic charts common to field guides. The mycological society recently performed a play there riffing on Doctor Faustus, in which nerds portrayed mushroom collectors haunting Faust, who sold his soul for a lifetime supply of morels. Now that's Coney.

Coney is the word I use to describe the grotesque and twisted, something so disturbing it's funny. Something New York, something convoluted, something ill-flowering, like a wart. A friend who just returned from China was telling me over a shrimp dinner that markets in Beijing sell grubs-on-a-stick. That's Coney. He handed me a menu he'd lifted from this Beijing restaurant called *Escape Mushroom Style* that listed fifteen pages of mushroom-based dishes—our collective reverie—minus one page of various sheep dick entrees. Coney.

I used to peddle organic produce at health food conventions. Frequently, my booth was across from the reishi booth, always the most sparsely attended table. Littered with finger-like, brown, red, and orange striated conchs alongside pamphlets printed in Mandarin, the reishi table was considered by most to be mysterious and sketchy.

"Is that a mushroom cult?" people whispered as I fluffed up kale bundles.

Reishi contains anti-cancer agents, and is a detoxifier that has been used in tea, powder, and extract form for thousands of years. It's a preventative. I was confused about why people avoided eye contact with the reishi promoters, as if looking at or thinking about cancer cure would promote neoplastic growth. Aversion to disease and the oddities surrounding it is weak. One cannot stay well without facing illness. Camped next to these mushroom enthusiasts for days straight, I read their literature, heard the miracle tales, and thanked Coney I didn't have cancer. Chinese medicine is righteous. I stored the mushroom's healing potential in the back of my mind, like a chestnut.

It was during this healthy period that I selected Scruffles from a box of barking pups. His spotted paws won me over. A proud new pet owner, I headed to the local bookstore and bought pet books with wolf covers to study canine acupuncture and flower remedies. At the time, I lived three thousand miles away. For over ten years now, Lolly and I have taken turns parenting this dignified canine.

Thursday after the Wonder Wheel tears, I took Scruffles to a Chinese herbalist in Manhattan. She had shiny auburn hair, and her hands and arms were ringed with silver and copper jewelry. She smelled friendly, like bok choy fried in ylang-ylang.

"He looks really well otherwise," she said. I inhaled her positivism as I would a fresh chanterelle.

"How long does he have?" I asked, grasping my tissue just in case.

"Years if the herbs work," she said. "But you must remove that tumor soon."

"Tuesday," I said, committing to a date. She was the doctor to trust.

We left with a sack of herbal tinctures, a list of foods Scruffles could eat, and recipes for his home-cooked meals. Scruffles and I now eat the same stew: poultry laced with turmeric, sea salt, carrots, and other "cooling" veggies. Twice daily he gets syringes full of serums, multi-vitamins disguised as cheese powder, and Indian rhubarb extract alternating with aloe vera juice poured into his purified water. Bad tap water may have caused all this. When Scruffles was young, I put citrine and smoky quartz crystals in his water bowl, at least, and hoped for the best. Nowadays, I dose both of us with everything because it can't hurt. We are on a permanent wellness kick.

I process trauma in unproductive ways. I twiddle my fingers, or apply lipstick only to immediately remove it. I cook food and forget to eat it. After deciding against radiation, which meant thousands of dollars and a month of anesthetizing the dog several times per week, all my dreams cropped up stinkhorn. Those putrid mushrooms that I most detest because they look like dog dicks, sprouted out of Scruffles' coat, appeared in salads and stir-fries I ate. Came out in the tap with the water.

Years ago, when I toured the Kew Gardens mycology archive, the director opened one of Charles Darwin's herbals and displayed a 150-year-old stinkhorn. He told me that Darwin's daughter considered it pornographic. Cancer is Coney porno. I couldn't translate these stinkhorn visions. I hoped the visions meant that Scruffles' pain was transferring into me. Healing is exorcism, a withdrawal and transference of the unwanted. I wanted to be the medicine woman who could kill, neutralize, and dissipate my dog's mutating cells. Step one was to physically remove the growth; step two was to escape the Coney.

Two weeks after the procedure, Scruffles and I drove north to the foot of the mountain where Van Winkle passed out on ale. I called Lolly on cellular from the rock Rip might have napped on and explained a theory.

"Tie some feathers in your hair," I said. "Crow, eagle… anything but pigeon. The feathers will fortify you."

"You're regressing," Lolly said. "I haven't heard these mystical hippie theories since you were a vegetarian ten years ago."

"Look," I said. "Feathers can't hurt. Put them on your dashboard if you can't bear wearing them."

There's a comical scene in *I Love You, Alice B. Toklas*, when Peter Sellers shows up in a fringed leather jacket for his conservative brother's tuxedo wedding. He's covered in feathers, and the movie is one big happy ending from there.

"We're talking on cell phones," Lolly said. "Feathers are retro."

"Is Rip Van Winkle too retro for you?" I asked.

I considered chucking my phone into the stream running five feet over where Scruff was drinking. A woodpecker hacked at an elm tree. I'd have to email everyone for their numbers again, plus I couldn't talk to Lolly. The golden handcuffs.

"Your cell phone is probably giving you cancer right now," Lolly said.

"Luddite," I said.

"Aren't you the Luddite, avoiding the city? Call me when you forgive civilization," Lolly said. "I'll be at the bar with my scotch on the rocks."

I didn't lodge in a tee pee. I shacked up in a Catskills dive motel. A junky walked laps around the building, and whole families manned lawn chairs on the motel room porches. A pimp ran girls between his grass green sedan and his room. I had mushroom guides sprawled out on the bed, where Scruff and I watched M*A*S*H reruns.

"Feeling okay?" I asked him, petting him beside me on the bed. Every time I looked at him my eyes went automatically to his shaved crotch, and I felt nasty. His six-inch stapled incision looked clean and was healing properly.

Scruffles smiled and hung his tongue out. He was tired from hiking. I refilled his bowl of water and set it beside him.

Next morning we headed out early. We didn't see Rip as I'd hoped, but it was a breezy autumn day and planks crossed wet meadows to preserve plant life. Mushrooms sprouted on every dead tree trunk: oysters, maitake, sulfur shelf. Scruffles peed on rocks as we bushwhacked up a ravine. We shared turkey sandwiches again in that special hemlock grove.

My cell phone sounded so out of place. West Coast: I answered.

"Will you accept a collect call from L.A. County Jail?" an operator asked.

Lolly was drunk driving, hit a fire hydrant and a lady at a bus stop. Luckily, only her leg was broken.

"How do you run over a leg?" I asked.

"I don't remember," Lolly said. "She has a leg cast. I need five grand," Lolly said.

"That's my feather money," I said. "I want to show Scruffles a good time instead of radiation."

"I'm in prison!" Lolly said.

"Give me a minute to think," I said. Scruff's ears were perked up, ready to think too.

"Good boy," I said. "Find some money." Mr. Van Winkle's buried treasure?

Money-wiring plans were made, and I folded my phone shut, slid it into my pocket. Coney phone. The woods and the city are the same some days. If bad news was bricks, I'd live in a fortress.

Scruffles licked my calf. I threw some rocks and packed it up.

On the path back, Scruffles located a shiny polypore whose skin actually reflected sunlight. It was a brown-red conch with ochre stripes edging its rim. Reishi? Different from the brown, whose velveteen skin you can carve pictures into. I snapped it off the tree trunk and carefully put it in my pack to shoot and ID later.

The nearest Catskills bail bonds place was across from Kozy Kitchen, a Coney diner decorated with baskets of silk flowers and gingham fabrics. I wired all the cash I had in the world and planted myself in a booth for coffee. Scruffles was tied up outside. Cranked on caffeine, I then wandered down the block to the scented candle shop to soothe myself with the smell of beeswax until Lolly called with release news. My sibling is loveable but he gets sailor-style drunk. One D.U.I. ago, he fell asleep at the wheel and drove into some park's tennis courts. I get jealous of people who rest assured that if they go unconscious someone will be there to help. Scruffles would rescue me, if he could.

The dog and I stopped for one more overnighter on the way back to Coney. I was broke now, and I wanted to show Scruffles one last good time. He wags his tail at motel room doors and stares at their doorknobs until I let him in. Then he jumps on the bed and readies himself for television. Knowing he truly appreciates my meager gifts brings me joy. I charged the motel on my credit card just to get this reaction out of my dog, which must say something bizarre about me.

"You're blocking the view," I said, on the king-size with Scruffles as the sun set, watching nature documentaries. During commercials we took turns with the remote; he can change channels if he paws it hard enough. How will I face life without this guy? I took the polypore out to identify it. It was glossier than *Ganoderma applanatum*, the reishi I knew. *Soft, corky, flat, zoned, red-varnished cap with white to dull brown pores… in its stalked form, this is the ancient Chinese 'mushroom of immortality,' also called the 'herb of spiritual potency.'* Red reishi, or Ling Chih: *Ganoderma lucidum.* An even better anti-cancer.

"You found Ling Chih," I said. "Good dog."

Scruffles licked his chops. Coneylicious. Fortified for impending night, it was back to the city in the morning with red reishi and my Frankenweenie.

JACKPOT (II)

This was the most in-demand tree. Every man with a machete had for centuries been dying to cut it down or to hack it up a little bit. The people who had historically succeeded in chopping it kept branches in their houses as trophies to show they dominated something super old. These guys, according to the sign chained around the trunk listing violation penalties for petting the tree or even looking at it wrong, were called Tree Poachers. There were guilty female culprits, too, though most women smuggled smaller pieces home to boil in tea or to chew superstitiously.

Most people in town respected the tree and, for the most part, went about their daily business in kindhearted ways. But there was something about the tree that brought out humanity's sinister side. It had the power of something 800 years old. At 200 feet tall, it would have made good lumber except for its numerous burls. From under it, one could barely see the sky, though bald spots were apparent since many of the tree's main arteries had been severed in the last century. The tree was stubby with sappy branch wounds whose fresh scent disguised the stench of its stagnant swamp surroundings.

This conifer, lodged in dank Mexican jungle, even looked swampy with drooping needles and twigs sagging off bigger branches like water-logged churros. Dry to the touch, the tree shed soft papery bark whose feathery, drenched appearance made it look like it had eternally soaked in standing water. The tree looked more like a pathetic willow than Mexico's most revered pine.

Tourists came daily to snap photos of themselves standing with the tree. Local bums loved loitering in the town square, but the grass was boggy and the town-elected Tree Patrol issued pricey vagrancy tickets. The tree-saving movement here was ironically impassioned. Sappy stumps where branches should be, they said, made the tree susceptible to swamp rot. Shop owners, who comprised the movement's majority, were especially invested in the tree's survival since tree memorabilia was their livelihood. But even the most avid tree guardians were compelled to midnight tree slashing. No one knew why the tree provoked the town's sadistic streak.

Huevito and Florencita were a married couple who some nights had no better idea than to go to town with their machetes to splinter up the very thing that put their landscape on the map. In this village, their birthplace, they lived four blocks from the tree but only two blocks from the iron railing that protected the tree and its root system.

The lovers wore ski masks when sneaking over the fence in the wee hours. They'd pass a bottle of aguardiente back and forth, and start stabbing. Huevito cut all dangling burls or branches off. Since one of his household pastimes was machete sharpening, one or two hard chops with his fine blades sliced nubs clean off. He got running starts and twirled like a samurai. His performances inspired Florencita, who stood way back to appreciate his interpretive dances.

She, on the other hand, had spent many an evening carving pictures of skulls and naked ladies onto the tree's bosom as if tattooing an old friend. Huevito rarely complimented her on this art. She deliberately didn't nickname the tree, because she didn't want to fall in love with it. She and Little Egg had TP'ed the tree as kids. Their adult romance had blossomed in this tree's presence. In their living room, they kept a shrine's worth of vivisected tree parts. She was attached enough.

Huevito, dubbed Little Egg by his father because he was the

last of four boys and a whole foot shorter than them, cut the tree because it made him feel bigger. For example, he couldn't be a masseuse with such small hands, and he couldn't be a professional wrestler. Worse, he was never trained as a tree pruner, his childhood aspiration.

Florencita loved his smallness, and the tree made her feel like fucking Little Egg because it complemented Huevito's pugnacious side. She thought of Little Egg as scrambled or sunny side up, while under the tree he became hard-boiled. Flo normally succumbed to tedious housework, so to her the tree symbolized everything besides cooking and cleaning. She had never done ladylike things, like erotic dancing, because most men thought she was a dogface. And this was slightly true; Flo had a large, lumpy nose, missing front teeth, and lard rolls ruffling her midsection.

On Easter Sunday, Florencita got fed up with washing laundry, dishes, and their horse, Feo, whose hooves got so caked with swamp mud on rides that he could hardly gallop. Since the first day of spring, Huevito and Feo had been out with the metal detector, combing the countryside for submerged weaponry. He coveted gold, copper, silver, any metal really, especially in sword form. Chances of discovering metal were slim because there had been only one significant battle here and the loot was way raided. Metal detecting and horse bathing were not generating major income. When Huevito came home with a mud-encrusted horse and two rusty coins that were not only *not* antique but also too disintegrated to buy groceries, Flo waved her finger at him, "Get a real job!"

"Why don't you?" Little Egg snarled, polishing the coins with his t-shirt.

"This swamp stinks," Flo said. "And there's no work here."

"I'm hungry," Little Egg said.

It was going to be one of those days.

But that night, Little Egg grabbed two newly sharpened machetes while Flo got out a paring knife, a switchblade, and a slender sword Huevito affectionately called her Lady'chete. Stealthily, they tiptoed over to the tree's iron railing, upon which hung a sign hand-painted in cursive: *Forbidden to Cut Parts of the Tree.* They'd memorized the way each letter looped righteously upwards. Pausing to read, then hopping the fence, was a ritual that made Flo and Little Egg reverential but devilish, apologetic but elated.

Sphinx moths flitted about like teeny dollar bills. Stray cats squatted on every branch, hissing at each other. Little Egg and Flo arranged their knives on the ground as if hosting a yard sale. Each blade glinted in full moonlight from different angles, reminding Flo of diamonds and Huevito of power tools. Flo leaned over to kiss Huevito as he fondled the biggest machete.

Huevito used his blade gorilla-style, but watching Little Egg whittle fresh growth this time wasn't doing it for Flo. She observed her husband flying around like an enraged ape and realized that her sultry hatch marks weren't cutting it, figuratively speaking. Her small marks weren't as boldly gestural as his war dance. Her routine would be more radical, she concluded, if she physically ignored the tree and cut it, instead, with her mind.

"Huevito," she called. "Watch this."

Flo picked up Lady'chete and ran it along the tip of her tongue. Little Egg was too turned on to tell her to stop, even when a little blood pooled in her mouth. He picked up a tree branch and fingered its frothy pine needles. When the licking was over, Flo put the sword down and took off her sneakers before stepping barefoot on it.

"No!" Huevito said, half-heartedly. "Don't..."

Arms out, she looked like a tightrope walker. The mud helped the blade stand erect.

Little Egg imagined, in close-up, the shiny blade making

provocative slices on his wife's feet. It dawned on him that he had been cutting the tree all these years because he enjoyed seeing it suffer. A revelation. For a split second, Little Egg cared more for the tree than for Flo's feet. *Maybe all along,* Huevito thought, *I loved the tree more than my wife.*

"Ouch!" Flo yelled, jumping off the Lady'chete. She looked down and saw her right foot bottom gashed the long way. "Help," she said, as she began to sob.

Huevito took his shirt off and tied it around her foot. Coins began to rain down from the tree's expansive canopy. Flo and Huevito let them accumulate before deciding whether or not they should start rolling in cash, but it appeared that these were only wooden nickels. Florencita sobbed more. They made umbrellas over their heads with their arms. Little Egg yelled through the downpour, "Fill your fanny pack just in case!"

"You fill it," Flo sniffled. "My foot hurts."

Little Egg grabbed her pack and shoveled coins in. When it bulged, they hobbled home.

The next morning, Huevito attributed the windfall to his tree-maiming epiphany, while Florencita wondered if the tree had tipped her for seductive dancing. They debated over fresh ham and eggs Huevito had purchased earlier with the wooden nickels. They had covered the wound with cotton and tied it shut with string in lieu of paying for stitches, and her foot was propped up on a chair.

"Let's cut back on tree cutting," Huevito said.

"But it might make us rich," Flo said.

"To thank us for not cutting it," Huevito said.

"Or because it finds me sexy," she said.

"Either way," Flo said, "we should get out there in case it rains again." Later that day, to prepare, she put on her best lingerie—a faded tiger-striped camisole with shot elastic—under her sweat pants. She planned to buy new dancing underwear with the coins this time, wooden or not.

It was midnight when Little Egg and Flo went to coax more coins out of the tree. Flo hopped on one foot, using Huevito as a crutch. She'd spent all day mentally choreographing a blade dance that involved zero stepping on sharp edges. Huevito lifted her over the railing, and Flo stripped. Perched on one leg like a flamingo, she twirled her Lady'chete baton-style and sliced figure eights above her head.

Little Egg watched impatiently. He wanted coins but didn't believe this was the way to get them, plus he wanted her to stop for romance under the tree.

Any day now, Flo thought, breaking a sweat.

"Give it a rest," Little Egg said, irritated. He picked up his own machete and lopped off a couple of branches out of sexual frustration.

It was then that metal coins poured down. Flo saw Little Egg hacking and felt confused, but it seemed to work so she started in too. They took turns hewing, like loggers alternating axes. Some coins were Easter egg hued. Half piñata, half piggy bank, the tree rained coins until the whole thing crackled and fell over, taking out a corner store and an electrical pole on the way down. Stuffing a few sacks full of coins, Flo and Huevito limped home as Tree Patrol sirens sounded at the other end of the town square. Home, they spilled the coins on the living room carpet and counted, forgetting that they'd just felled this money tree.

In the morning, the community assembled around the stump. The Tree Patrol Commissioner gave a tragic speech and women cried into their handkerchiefs. Men with chain saws started clearing debris. *Let's punish who did this*, a shop owner said. A mob formed to march door-to-door. Huevito and Florencita rode the bus one town over to the swap meet, to buy Flo new underwear with their nickel cache.

"The tree will open up to me," Flo said to Huevito, as they leafed through piles of panties at the open-air market.

"The tree is dead," Little Egg declared solemnly. When Flo heard that, she added the sassiest panties—red ruffles—to her purchase pile.

The couple danced and cleaved the stump with machetes nightly. Nothing worked. They were fighting constantly about how to get more coins, or how to at least rejuvenate their beloved. Finally, three weeks after the tree's debris had been cleared, Florencita got stinking drunk and snuck out alone to dry-hump the tree stump in her red ruffles. It even seemed ridiculous to her, but the tree had been her first tipping client. For the first time, she felt like a real stripper.

A couple songs into her lap dance, coins started flying at her not from above but from the side. She shined her flashlight and found Little Egg, tossing coins from behind a rose bush.

"You hit the jackpot, baby," Florencita yelled.

As soon as she said this, more coins started flying from the sidelines again. The Tree Patrol shined spotlights on the couple and began a coin-hurling contest.

"Surrender," they yelled through a bullhorn.

"It's my stump!" Flo yelled. She hurled coins so hard they sliced the police. Tree Patrol crawled away, injured. Flo wanted coins, but only from her deceased tree. *The one I cut down*, she thought, *mi amor.*

From then on, people threw coins at Florencita everywhere she walked, and called her a tree slut. She couldn't blame them. In the end, it was the deceased tree that made all the money, which it stored in its bank account also known as Swamp Mud. When the scandal blew over, though, Huevito took Flo instead of Feo to rob the mud bank with his metal detector. Flo vowed never to wash that muddy horse again.

WAR FOODS

"Let's go downtown and get some government cheese," my father used to say to my brother and me. He thought that was entertainment enough for the weekends he had us in his custody. He was an ex-Marine who had served two tours in Vietnam. We didn't need the cheese, because we weren't that poor, so he must have thought we liked waiting in line to get five-pound cubes of Kraft Military Velveeta with the rations coupons he got from working at the Veteran's Administration. Carrying that 12x4x4-inch brown cardboard box marked with code numbers and the word CHEESE in capital letters was almost as humiliating as getting picked up from private school in his government-issued tan Ford Pinto that backfired. He used to say, "Don't worry about all those stuck-up kids. Be glad you're not like them."

But eating that cheese just felt wrong.

Sometimes I ate the cheese if no one else was watching. It had a doll-head flavor. I'd cut rubbery slices off the end of the block with a cheese wire and throw them onto bread for a grilled cheese sandwich. "Don't you want some salt on that?" my dad would ask, tapping the salt shaker above the browning bread. Then, he'd open the door of his tiny hotel fridge and drink some pickle juice out of the jar. If the cheese ran over the sides of the bread while grilling, it would never burn or sizzle. It just liquefied and re-congealed like candle wax. You could melt it, pour it onto your hand, and watch it turn into a chunk again. Every time I ate the cheese I felt like a dog bent over a bowl of kibble.

Dear Annette, this letter reads, emailed twenty years after my father's death. *If this is you, then hello, I am your cousin, daughter of your father's sister. We have not heard from you since your father's funeral...* I stare at the screen, read the letter eight times. I don't remember much about the funeral, especially the cousins, but I do remember burying my coveted black hi-top Converse All Stars in my dad's casket. The smelly sneakers are probably still in that grave. I still can't put faces on my cousins.

Death is an exercise in lucidity or lack thereof, a test of the memory's elasticity. What will I remember of this person, and what will I do with that information? Why did I forget everything else? I remember the gap between my dad's two front teeth, but not his eyes. No more am I surrounded by stuck-up kids, no more boring days trapped in my dad's cramped apartment flipping through his record collection. How does opening this letter still induce in me that feeling of being force fed the cheese? This relative of mine sincerely reaching out gives me one more thing to be embarrassed about: my lousy memory.

But I am more thrilled about the prospects of having family. I call my brother after a tenth read.

"Guess who emailed me?" Like he could. "Our cousin," I say. "Remember all those cousins we have?"

We struggle to recall them. One caused a family feud at the funeral because he got my dad's pick-up truck, the only possession of monetary value. I got my dad's war medals, which I somehow managed to lose. My brother remembers one of our cousins smelling like salami.

"Should I try to see her?" I ask him, about the cousin who wrote.

"Sure, Annette," he says.

The only date I recall with my aunt, this cousin's mom, was to the Rosicrucian church to see mummies. Over a hotdog lunch afterwards, we got a lesson in Egyptian afterlife. We don't care how eccentric they are or were; it's lucky we have a family. At this point, I'd pay top dollar for any memories of my dad.

"I'll make a lunch date," I say before we hang up.

Then, there was my embarrassment at dad's house. He didn't have duck or golf paintings, he had one watercolor of the World War I flying ace, Red Baron. Instead of a pool table room full of beer signs, lapis lazuli globes, shoehorns, and other Father's Day crap, he had a ramshackle room with one fraying orange armchair and a homemade plywood bookshelf. For washing hands, he used gritty Lava soap instead of musky man-scented mall soaps like Sandalwood or Spice. Rather than the preppy upper-class tortoiseshell and brass brushes my friends' dads used to comb their hair, he had the kind of plastic comb you buy at the gas station—the type called combbrush with a flat-toothed surface and a three-fingered slot on top for maximum control. I pleaded with him to get a real mirror in the bathroom. He said all we needed was a 3x4 emergency mirror, the tinny metal kind you take camping. I was a teenage girl. My girlfriends had track-lit three-angle mirrored vanities to primp in. I wasn't that picky, I just wanted a mirror.

One day, I learned why my dad hated mirrors. Dad was in the bathroom, finishing his shower, and I was in the living room when I heard his scream-grunt.

"Hunnnhh, hunnh!" Then the bathroom door slammed open. The apartment was dinky, and I was already at that bathroom's door. Little did my dad know that I was now prepared to drive him to the hospital if necessary. I'd practiced driving illegally and was well versed in stick shifting by age thirteen, from having given older friends sober rides home. I was ready to yank that skinny canvas cot I hated sleeping on right out of the bedroom, to drag Dad, unconscious, out to the car if need be. I would be his ambulance.

"Dad!" I said, putting my hand on his shoulder. "What happened?"

He stood there, silent, pale, still groping the little mirror. His beard stubble made him look deranged.

"Bad daydream," he said, inhaling deeply. He set the handheld mirror down on the sink's edge, and walked out of the bathroom into the bedroom to lie down. I followed him into bed.

"What was it about?" I asked.

"The war," he said.

I didn't press him, and instead went into the kitchen to bring him back some water. He had seen something terrible in that mirror. From then on, I didn't pester him to install one.

A few years ago I found a manila envelope of papers I kept, containing letters and notes he wrote, his handwriting samples. He had angular writing, like an architect's: neat, slanting forward to the right, penmanship marked with speed and purpose. I know that folder of his papers intimately, but I had never seen this poem of his in there. How and when had it been slipped in? I read it, again and again, trying to remember when he gave it to me, and if he really wrote it. Though his printing is proof of authorship, I have difficulty reconciling the poem's content with that person I loved.

No one escapes death
Hoped and believed in the world beyond death
Try to change the facts
Why fear death?
In order to live one must nearly die
Try to communicate with the dead
Life includes death
The Lord of Misfortune
Beyond the threshold of our ordinary experience
Cataclysmic journey from birth to death

Old terrors mingle with old truths
Death rides a Pale Horse
Ecstatic convulsions
Smell out the demon with snakes for feet
Sudden death from sheer terror is not unknown
He feigns to abstain from death
Exquisite torments
The taint of diabolical possession

Was it Death he saw in that tin mirror? My dad died two years later.

Beyond the cheese, the government-issued Salisbury steaks tasted a little bit sweeter than dog food, like Alpo mixed with sugar and slapped into patties. Smell some Alpo and you'll know how it tasted—like horse and cow scraped off the floor of a meat-packing plant after men have stomped in it. The steaks came in slender olive-green boxes that contained sealed baggies with meat encased in a jellied aspic sauce. The box had SALISBURY STEAK in the same lettering as the cheese. The sauce may have had tomatoes in it, but they were hard to detect due to its uniform russet color. You could eat the steak or poo it out, and it would look pretty much the same except for having been transformed into a log. Poo has that intestinal flavor as well—I've never tried it, but the smell tells you. It's the smell that goes, *I am not only unfit for human consumption, I am unfit for anything in the animal kingdom.* This is food that only microbes should be eating.

My dad reserved the "poo steaks" for fishing trips to Lake Isabella. This summer trip, the lakeshore was clouded with mosquitoes. We were in the bush—canvas army tent, rations boiling in the plastic baggies over the fire, lantern burning white gas, and our dad slathering us with insect repellent. My brother thought this way of living would aid him if he ever got stranded in the jungle. He even got his pocket knife out and carved X's into his bug bites, then sucked out the blood, like our father had taught him. It was all very Vietnam—like a POW had taken his children into hiding and was briefing us on stratagems. I wondered if my dad had ever been tortured, had his wrists tied down and bamboo slivers pushed under his fingernails. Had he ever been forced to eat rats? No, but he'd told me once how he'd taken his camera on a photo shoot of severed Viet Cong heads, and he'd showed me a picture of an old lady who'd had her eyes poked out by soldiers. Not by anyone he knew, but he'd felt compelled to commemorate her.

On the first night of this camping trip, Dad woke us up in our tent, shouting, "I'll see you in hell!" The next morning, feeling guilty, he let my brother and I paddle all over the lake while he picked at his teeth with toothpicks on the lakeshore, fishing for catfish. In our canoe, I told my brother that our dad was a Pirate of War—a different kind of POW.

I ate the steak that night because I was starving. I'd been rowing all day. My dad pulled the sack of meat out of the fire with the point of his rosewood-handled hunting knife and slit open the plastic, plopping the slop into my mess kit pan. I unfolded my aluminum fork and bravely dove in. I couldn't bear to chew my bites; I just placed them as far back in my throat as possible and swallowed.

My girlfriends back home were probably at some fancy steak house, while their parents sipped martinis and flashed their jewelry. Whenever I ate with these families and saved my meat to take home in a doggy bag, glances shot back and forth between the parents. *Does she have enough to eat at home?* I can't wrap my mind around people who are embarrassed to take good food home. What a paltry thing to be embarrassed about. I had different food embarrassments. This camp steak, for example. It tasted grainy, like it had been stored in the attic with the wartime memorabilia and the musty furniture. My dad must have been saving these rations since he was released from duty in 1974.

"So, did you meet the cousin?" my brother asked after I returned from the road trip I took to meet the cousin.

"No," I said. "I just can't handle it. The whole food thing…"

"Food thing?" he asked.

"The lunch idea was too much," I said.

"Why didn't you meet her for a walk in the park, then?" he asked.

"I don't know what to talk about," I said.

"Kids, careers," he said.

"You're welcome to," I said. "I can't do it yet."

My brother hung up, baffled. But as of today, he hasn't gone to meet our cousin either.

I went to fix myself a sandwich in the kitchen. Birds tweeted out the window, teetering on the branches of a guava tree. They chipped their beaks at the budding fruits to get at ripening tidbits. Birds don't need to wait for fruits' full sweetness; they savor every stage. My PB&J sandwich did the job. Will I ever take an interest in food preparation? I'm a terrible cook. I eat to survive, ever since my dad served me those gnarly Salisbury Steak rations. Choke it down and move on. I miss my dad, and this petty remembrance of him doesn't make me proud.

Don't eat government-issued foods unless you are a prisoner of war. Don't eat Velveeta; use it for fishbait. Don't eat boxed meat. These foods are last resorts if you're out of grocery money or trapped in earthquake rubble. Eating sick things when it's not necessary is like watching people agonize over gunshot wounds. I guess this diet was gratifying for a soldier who wanted to reminisce, but it was boring and confusing for his offspring. Re-hashing desperate times doesn't compute with children who haven't had desperate times.

War pirates like my father make sure their kids know they have it easy, but not in the conventional way. They shell-shock the young with the grotesque. I was taught to be grateful for the war foods because my dad lived on them for two years straight. I wouldn't insult his patriotism. I was glad I had a dad who weathered that war to feed me. But will I always be a dog eating kibble?

SHRUB OF EMOTION

I used to be a dolphin trainer, and drove to work in a black swimsuit and flip-flops. My office was a bench next to the pool. I sported a clipboard and waterproof work supplies. The dolphins could fetch, jump through hoops, score goals in water polo, and were advanced synchronized swimmers. With a whistle and some hand signals, I could tell them to circle the perimeter of their pool, pick up a disc and chuck it to me like a Frisbee, then come over for mackerel. Dolphins can handle a string of up to twenty commands.

Getting to know porpoises will convince any skeptic that animals can talk. That's why it didn't seem far-fetched to me when this sprout I germinated began to make noise. I just brought it into a quiet corner of the house so its sounds would bounce off the walls and be magnified.

My weed's first word was *water.* It took me a week to figure out what she was saying. It sounded like a two-syllable high-pitched hum: *mra mur.* It could have been a fly talking. Since then her voice has deepened. By the time she was a month old, she could say in elfin intonation, *Get these gnats off me.*

I took my leafy friend along to my new home because this is no ordinary plant. Sure, I will smoke her when she reaches maturity, but in the meantime she has been teaching me what it means to be herbaceous. I see her wilt with fatigue or perk up when misted. I nicknamed her The Shrub of Emotion.

Since when did it take hours for my bush to form a sentence? Maybe it was because we were on the airplane, and my potted friend disliked cabin pressure. Maybe she was shy. For a female bush, she is easily intimidated. Someone gave me a look from across the aisle. For a minute, I didn't know why.

"*Ohh.* They think I'm talking to myself," I said. My weed was making me look bad.

It was like this for the duration of the flight. I kept her in a duffle bag under my seat, so only her leaves peeked out. Don't ask me how I weaseled my way through customs.

My shrub and I escaped the airport and taxied two hours to our new rural Swiss abode. She was back to her chatty self after requesting an extra dose of fertilizer. *Put me in the window sill*, she said, *that artificial light was torture.*

My emotional shrub forms sentences by bending her stems and buds into a series of squeaks, wheezes, and bursts of air. She sounds like a child mimicking a choo choo train. I can hear her plainly now, being well attuned to her needs, but I might offer you an ear trumpet to magnify her words until they become recognizably audible. As with any new language, her creaks and whispers are foreign jumble until you learn the words. It's a mistake for humans to personify plants, but it's also a mistake to assume plants don't try to communicate with us.

Translated to English, this town is called Milk of the Wise Man. This rented farmhouse in the Alps is clean and sparse. Its windows crank open and closed, and exposed wooden beams line the ceiling. The bathtub used to be a trough—hopefully no livestock had used it as their hot tub. I bathed and put on a nightgown, even though it's still light out. It's tweaky how the sun doesn't set until midnight. This residency will be a challenge. A neighbor just dropped off a strudel.

Goats are roaming through my yard. I'm here on a grant to study how alpine flora and fauna feel about living above the tree line. Do rams enjoy it when their horns ice up? Is living on the side of a cliff satisfying? Do ferns like having their brackens pelted by hailstones? I have lists of questions, and a trunk full of equipment to record and transcribe my wildlife interviews. My grant application was entitled: *Middleman.* My main duty, as I see it, is to ease negotiations between the plant and animal kingdoms.

It all started with a choking Sinaloan donkey. My boyfriend at the time and I stopped to help it. We were in a dusty marketplace, traveling in a border town below the Rio Grande. There were donkeys all over, standing idly, packed with heavy loads. This donkey's owner yelled for help as his donkey coughed something up. I wasn't dying to put my fingers down that animal's throat.

When I finally grabbed a stick and inserted it into the donkey's mouth as my boyfriend, Francis, held its jaws open, a baggie full of seeds fell out. The donkey gasped for air and we gave it some water. People clapped and the owner—not the donkey—yee-hawed. No one wanted to touch the seed pouch, so I snatched it up, rinsed it off, and pocketed it.

"Yuck," Francis said. He was wearing walking shorts and rope sandals, so with his big beard he looked like a saint.

"See how they're bundled?" I asked. "Someone was smuggling them."

"Drugs," Francis said. He always restated the obvious. Sometimes I admired this, but this time it was annoying.

These Donkey Seeds reminded me of small jumping beans. Would they grow donkeys?

Francis and I were taking a trip to forget that we were sick of each other. When we met, I loved his gentle demeanor and simple approach to complicated topics, like love. "I love you," he'd say. "That's all that matters." He wasn't sidetracked by excess psychological baggage. He never doubted my intentions, for example. But his idealistic naïvete irked me. I felt like hurting him. When it started affecting our sex life, I decided it was time for a vacation.

To my mind, these seeds added a lot of excitement to an otherwise dull trip. I brought the seeds home with me, in hopes that they'd continue to work their mojo on our life together, which needed spicing up.

I snuck the seeds across the border in my bra, and then germinated them in wet paper towels. Day by day, I'd enter the kitchen and find another sprout dead. But my Shrub of Emotion was thriving. By the time I transferred her into soil, she told me that if I harvested her in a year, I could smoke her for a pleasant high. Francis the Skeptic came over to see her.

"I don't hear *her* talking, if it's a her," he said.

"She only talks at night, and it is a *her* because her hairs are crossed," I told him. (If the hairs point straight out, you've got a boy, and if they make an X, it's a girl.)

"I think you already smoked her," he said.

"Stoners can't train dolphins," I said. "But this is an exception. If a plant tells me to smoke it, I'd be dumb not to. It's my scientific obligation."

"You're spending too much time with dolphins," he said.

"They're the only other animal besides the bonobo that has sex for pleasure," I said.

"If you'd rather have sex with a dolphin than with me, go right ahead," he said.

I was shocked that he stood up for himself. It made me like him more. For a split second, I thought that I'd made a mistake. He was a nice guy, the solid down-to-earth type. But that was the problem. You can re-evaluate somebody on the spot, but usually your previous assessments are correct. Someone can be wonderful and still not be right for you.

We don't keep in touch. I was sad, but the plant had already replaced him, in a way. I couldn't wait to roll up a fatty and taste her.

A few days after my split with Francis, Mike (the dolphin) tried to attack me underwater again, so I resigned. It was the fifth time this had happened, and each time my supervisor, Ron, said it was natural, even good, a sign that Mike accepted me as a true mate. Ron is a twirp; he probably likes getting accosted by dolphins. But I don't like being violently pumped from behind by a large rubbery creature. It's discomfiting and painful.

Ron offered me a sabbatical and recommended me for this grant. I packed my clothes and bought a ticket to Switzerland.

So here I am in this Swiss chalet. European life has its advantages. Each morning I eat cheese and bread, and feed Shrubbie with compost from a nearby turkey farm. Women hang clothes on twine clotheslines, and kids carry water buckets. Cows moo constantly, I guess because they're happy it's summer. The other day, I saw a man in lederhosen pulling a wagon full of chickens. Everyone here drinks beer and plays the accordion. There's a street festival dedicated exclusively to white asparagus. What century am I in? I've been thinking more about schnitzel than this science project.

Shrubbie suggested that while I wait for alpine animals to show up, I might research cannabis not only for her benefit, but to better my understanding of marijuana's magic. Here are selected excerpts from *The Alpine Weed Research Journal (dedicated to Shrubbie).*

Day One: Reading medieval herbals for hemp's medicinal cures. In Culpepper's *Complete Herbal* (1649), the seed emulsion, dropped into your ears, is said to "draw forth earwigs and other living creatures."

Day Two: I smoked a bit of Shrubbie. Snipped a bud with newly purchased Swiss Army knife. She winced. Went to sleep trying to decode words I imagined in scrambled cursive, words like *uphill* and *reinstated.*

Day Three: Read about Fitz Hugh Ludlow, 19th century American writer who documented his addiction to THC. Once sober, he satisfied his cravings for hash by blowing colored soap bubbles.

Day Four: Pruned Shrubbie. Sang her a birthday song, said, "Make a wish," and blew some candles out for her. Sometimes, when I smell Shrubbie, I get the munchies. But I so admire her palmate leaves and her strong pungent stems that I don't have the heart to kill her. Last night I told her I loved her. She is, at present, my closest friend.

Three months later, I've finally made owl contact. I think all it said is, *Stay away from my babies.* I stashed a dictaphone in its nest and caught its hoots on microcassette. When I played the tape for the lady next door, she seemed only momentarily impressed. It's easier for me to talk to animals than to the people here. Swiss-German sounds like spitting and rolling spoons on one's tongue. Maybe humans experience nature in the same way we experience being in a new country. I am merely skimming conversations. Are all humans missing 99% of the forest action? I don't feel like I'm missing that much when I hike.

Plants and animals communicate differently than humans, namely they don't hide their feelings. It's documented that animals and humans share emotions: rage, fear, curiosity, sexual attraction and lust, separations distress, social attachment, and happiness. But only humans can think ambiguously; only humans can have malintent towards something they love. I think about this when I think back to Francis. I loved him, but only sometimes.

Shrubbie loves me unconditionally. I know what Shrubbie needs because she's learned English. She needs a lot more than just water. Once she told me that she's lonely when I leave the house. Another time she said, *I'm so healthy, maybe I will live forever.* Her enunciation sounded like Haiku. That was our most poetic moment.

The fourth month into research, my first big breakthrough occurred with a pine marten. His coat was four kinds of brown.

Interview with *Edelmarder*

How old are you?

–Don't steal my nuts.

Do you like eating pinecones?

–I have cousins to feed. Don't steal my pinecones.

What was the saddest day of your life?

–I've learned three things from tragedy. One, keep your tail away from bicycle wheels. Two, buck teeth are nothing to mock. Three, there's a reason you never see martens at the beach.

Can I pet you?

–I climbed a tree once, to check my stash. Winter was coming. I heard bees leaving a nearby hive; they had their eyes on some sap I'd gathered. Soon, they surrounded me. They threatened me with their stingers. *Give up the sap*, they hummed. *Never*, I clicked back. A Sap War was brewing. Then I changed my mind. I put my tail up for a baby bee to rest on. I pet her, groomed her, and said to the queen, *Your baby is good. I'll trade my sap for her.* Plans were hatched, I raised her, and now I have a tamed bee colony and more honey than I can chug.

Do you have any regrets?

–I wish I could eat you.

I went home and played Shrubbie the tape. She swayed breezily when she heard it, claiming the marten sounded like a dolphin, so I checked to make sure I had the right tape in. We both had a good laugh. But then when I told her what the marten was saying, she said, *All that small mammals think about is their stash.*

You're my #1 stash, I thought. She wasn't my buddy anymore; Shrubbie was my object of desire. I wanted to devour her. She was dripping with sticky resin, and I wanted to cook her into a tray of brownies. I wanted to sizzle her in butter. *Whoa*, I thought, *I'm the witch in "Hansel and Gretel" and I'm already living in a gingerbread house.*

That time Shrubbie said she sought eternal life, was she trying to imply that she was too beautiful to harvest? Was that her way of begging for mercy? And what did she wish for on her birthday two months ago? Why did Francis have to be so nice? I never realized being too nice could make someone not love you anymore. My Shrub of Emotion was so ripe.

"I love you, Shrubbie," I said, clutching a pair of Swiss-made Precision Scissors. "But you know I have no choice."

THE SAD DRAG MONOLOGUES

Starring in order of appearance:

Chimney Sweep/Crackhead/Mime

Pink Hobo

Popcorn Maiden

Too Cute

The Fresh Prince/Black Pearl

Smoky E.L.F.

Koshare Wildcat

SMALL TIME SPENDER

I've noticed a new austerity floating around town like the ghost cocaine left behind. Austerity: eat that organic raw honey sparingly! Don't overdo that boutique goat cheese that roars at you like a lion from the fridge, *Cheese up in here, bitch, eat me!* Like what, you don't have an unlimited cheese budget? You don't drive around in your Porsche macking cave-aged gruyere? I'm over it. I'll live in the cave without cheese. I subsist on stardust now. Oh yeah, I lived on stardust back in the day. *Wait, specify stardust: uppers or enlightened matter?* In my new austere world I'm referring to the holy stuff, that which we consist of even though we think we're separate entities. *Drugs make the cave more fun, douche bag.* What business does pure cocaine have in a meditation cave? All alone with no one to talk to all night, no disco, no one to freak with on the dance floor? Remembering that night I danced perfectly with my hips in the West African funk circle at the nightclub. Remembering when I took a tumble down the stairs to drunkenly lament my friend's broken hip, the one he'd broken falling down stairs, then taxied back to where my man had returned early, furious, to grope the hotel room's toilet seat, barfing and huffing the minty designer shampoo sample for nausea relief. Remembering that time I did lines in the stretch Hummer and threw champagne glasses out the truck's sunroof. *That* was the opposite of austere. I'm talking about transcendence here, overcoming my intense desires. I've spent the past year apologizing and confessing. Just like how I write stories now, in poetic free verse, as if sentences are too decadent. All those words. *Parse it down; you talk too much.* I hope I have the flesh left to tidy these sentences up in the future, so I can call myself a storywriter instead of a poser poet, so I can call myself an author instead of a skeleton.

Austerity. I remember W.H. Auden wrote satirically about it, about the war, society, and other lofty topics. I read him in awe then, said, *I'll never beat Auden.* I wrote a prose paper about how Auden's poetry flogged me. I used wordy sentences, like tissues I'd blown my nose in, and hoisted them as my tattered white flag. And here I am, defeated again fifteen years later, eating trail mix for dinner, trying to be austere but failing miserably, pretending to be a poet but failing miserably. I'll turn this into a story so that no one knows it once tried to be a poem. No one will suspect that I paced around the room eating my meager cranberries and cashews pondering the meaning of life, feeling lonely because earlier, in the bathtub, I read about how the self is a falsity. The text warned me that I may feel like a balloon set free in the sky and that some who feel untethered by this message resort to nihilism. There is no self. I have my comforting turquoise desk lamp turned on and a sweet ska soundtrack, though, so I'm all right. I won't drift away. You can't pop me, universe! I might eat less or sleep less or feel compelled to leave those fancy pants behind when I covet them on a mannequin in Manhattan. I might shop for underwear in packs now because in my new austere universe lingerie isn't my number one priority. But sure, I'll admit I'm suffering because I wish I had a grand budget. Austerity is, at its basest, a cover-up: sad drag.

This austerity extends far outside me, though. My friends are sober now because they're out of drug money. One artist I know donned a robe in the form of a bed sheet and declared himself done with materialism. He'll be the canvas from now on. Performance art is totally in. I splurged on a five-dollar Barbie make-up kit to paint my face like Vishnu, and called the photos of my face art. But really it was just the goddess of boredom heckling me in the bathroom mirror, rearing her ugly rainbow face. Everyone's getting in on free hobbies like dream yoga.

We're starting to believe in the afterlife in hopes that the coke there will flow freely. Bardo will be our happy hour.

This austerity extends far beyond drug use, too. Home birth rates are up. Is that because women really want to have babies in their beds or because they can't afford the hospital? I know I for one don't want to pay some dude to pull a baby out of my vagina when I can do it for free on the front lawn. Men are jerking off to more refined fantasies, not to every half-baked pornographic whimsy after breakfast, lunch, and dinner. They pass this restraint off as Tantra. When I flip coins now to make decisions, I don't just drive to the beach to see dolphins if it's tails. I might save on gas and google porpoises instead. It's a thrifty universe. *Super cool brother, think you're a lover, but you'll discover you're just another brother.*

The all-loving, all-embracing, wise universe: the Jewel Tree Meditation is free! I finally understand where Ginsberg's lines came from! Hookers, wake up and realize that you don't need to give blowjobs in the park for this free deal you can get super high on. Enlightenment awaits us, in the form of Stevie Wonder. He's living with his hot wife in Detroit. Time to write a fan letter. Enlightenment wears dope sunglasses.

The tortoise who rationed her desert willow blossoms, and the prose writer who rationed these words, packing lines that originally slithered down the left margin in short cheapskate clusters—the greatest irony of all because poems use more paper—groove to Stevie together on their sandy patio while wondering when people will get rich again and how they will spend those riches after enduring austerity? When will monks grill porterhouse steaks at the Zendo? *You think you're cool, but you ain't cool no more.*

ORANGE

I can't help but see the pink juice in the syringe when I look out the window at my potted pelargonium, the flower my cat used to daintily sniff before I put her to sleep yesterday. There was that moment, after the shot, when her head relaxed, dropping into my cupped hand like an orange, and then the pink killed her within a minute. I was only bold enough to usher her out because the doctor told me the barbiturate would take her almost instantly. That didn't sound half bad. I wanted a shot too until I saw my kitty's pupils dilate and the doctor touched her eyeball to make sure she didn't blink. I thought of my mom and hoped for her health. Then I wanted to go home to ensure my husband and dog were still breathing.

I know animals don't live forever, but I wish they would. I wish all the pets I've had would hover around me to let me stroke their coats one last time. But then again, that would be creepy: simultaneously seeing all those members of my different lives. See, when I took a few moments to pet my cat's corpse, on one hand I lamented her death. But on the other, all of my living and dead snapped forward—and I understood the confusion of them crowding around me, spiritually overpopulating my brain with too much psychic baggage. If everyone and everything I loved were alive, life would be a labyrinth that led right back to where I started, here at this steel table, feeling abandoned by my cat, still with her eyes open, still her body warm but obviously emptied of its generous purring and miniature heartbeat mechanisms I used to press my ear up to her fuzzy belly to appreciate.

When I got home, I tearfully ate a banana and a phrase came to mind. *No one is your enemy; to hate others is to hate yourself. Desire causes mental poverty.* Then, I felt bad for wishing the dead to life, or for wishing to trade the dead for the living, for to wish is to disrespect the dead and myself. At that juncture, my wishes rearranged themselves into regrets for not having mummified my feline, as it would have been nice to be together in a stone tomb someday. Did the Egyptians have it right, letting the dead go only temporarily until they met again in the afterlife? Here I am, analyzing this pink poison. Is the pink juice in the syringe the Nile? There's a hole in the mummy theory. It's a fake-out like wishing the dead to life. How are two spirits who graduate into alternative matter ever going to meet up? The Egyptians were wishful thinkers. When we say goodbye, we won't see each other again. That's the hard part.

Sometimes people say to me, *we must have met in a previous life.* I'll take that fantasy today. Maybe I will meet you, tiny meow-head, in the next life. But I doubt it. I cry some more, and I put my banana down because I'm too sorrowful to eat fruit. Fruit is silly at a funeral. I lie on the floor and sob pathetically, demanding myself to stop guessing where my dead relatives went or how bad it will suck when my elderly dog departs, because those past and future anxieties are what I'm truly crying about. I dial my mother to say hello. My husband comes home and hugs me. Living in the present is best, and even heartbreak is okay.

MY PANDA EYES, MY SUNRISE

Since you moved out I've been living on popcorn. One bite at a time, telling myself this snack binge is a healthier addiction. I remember the football-sized jar of worms pickled in liquor at the agave farm, when I visited tequila's house in Oaxaca. On her porch, Sweet Reposado's, were cow-sized blue agave plants, desiccated like jerky, which is how I felt after I slammed several shots, rich idea-wise but as poor as a hand towel. I'd have some right now if I weren't shoveling an enormous bowl of popcorn into my mouth. To tequila, an underworld promontory, I've dedicated a costume: panda eyes for my past lucky days, my sunrise. Replacing tequila with popcorn is like switching a pal out with driftwood. What good is a log if it doesn't make the party so aggressive that it slaps you on the back? The grub is come, right? Semen? Wasn't it phallic that tequila farmers decided to praise their fat worms, selecting something maggoty to swallow that's high in protein? Sobriety is not going to be easy.

The day I visited the tequila farm was the day I felt as supreme as a Mixtec goddess, high on those Sierra Madre valley views, high on the clouds drifting through the cornflower-blue sky above the silver blue agave, it was so damn blue. Looking at the blue with you. Oaxaca: I played a flute and rolled in hibiscus blossoms to try to replicate that day on the farm, but nothing comes close. A photo can't touch that acrid stench of fermenting agave wafting out from the wooden well, where burros stirred twizzler sticks into a frothy ring to pulp the plant.

Tequila's summer lightning storm, boom! I knew if I didn't take that day by the reigns it would spank me with its prickly pear paddle. I started a fire after I licked every last pupa off the spiky, succulent leaves, and barely escaped because my passport was still alcoholic when I arrived at the airport. I have a headache remembering how horny I was. Popcorn works better than aspirin, but it doesn't bring back my libido. I haven't craved sex since the minute you walked.

I am lamenting the loss of two you's: you, lover and you, drink. I am not one to order my losses, sorting them into black and white like a skunk's tuxedo. Houndstooth is my mourning gown. I would like to wrap houndstooth around my head like a television-snow turban. Pile-driving popcorn into my mouth is like popping cassettes into a tape deck. I'll have just enough muscle left to peddle back out of the succulent's center. The road's yellow dividing line is a pollen-heavy stamen, along which I used to hunt that nectar, tequila, a very sickening syrup. Teosinte, corn's earliest relative, wedged itself into rocky crevices until humans realized that it could be tamed into something edible. Pre-corn to popcorn, the path of that plant usage has been illuminated. Today I might be a clown with sorry red rock star eyes, but tomorrow night I'll attempt to eject my rowdy claws to come find you, to haul you back.

THE CELEBRITY BEEKEEPERS

I was going to write about celebrity beekeepers. I'd been brewing an elaborate tale in my head for weeks about Solana, the diva, who only eats baba ghanoush and suns herself on patios while her bees feed on peach blossoms outside her bay window. And about Rhonda, the feisty one, who attends awards ceremonies in cocktail dresses with no underwear on beneath her skirts, and who prefers to strut on mirrored floors. And maybe there would be a man in there, just maybe one male beekeeper, a boy slave who keeps the bees organized, because Solana and Rhonda are preoccupied with being photographed from flattering angles. The innocent boy-child, with a clownish name like, oh, I don't know, Defithedra, something invented, because he is mythic basically, living in the shadow of the B-List celebs who call themselves beekeepers, while they wave their martinis around on the red carpet, though Defithedra does all the work. His name rhymes with Ephedra because he's always up, always keeping those bees in line, always cracking the whip on those ornery insects. Slave and slavedriver.

The diva and the slut move seamlessly through the night, at events of great importance, while their bees toil in wax, and the boy slave only occasionally gets paid because his employers always forget to cut him a check. They are forgetful because they are often flying on jets between countries, and who wants to write checks while seated on a private plane? Oops, they tell him, we left our checkbooks at home, and Defithedra can't pay his rent but he's so dedicated to the bees that he can't abandon them, for if he quits the bees will be orphaned, no one will recommend different pollens, no one will suggest they eat sage now, clover later. Rhododendron this afternoon? he asks his bees. Buckwheat bud? Thistle hair?

The bees need guidance. Bees need structure. They build honeycombs. Who would tell them what kind of honey to make if Defithedra left them? He works for a pittance, and the celebrity beekeepers take all the credit for the petite jars of honey they pass out at dinners, galas, and benefit brunches.

I was going to write a story about the three-tiered employee pyramid in which ladies hoard acknowledgments that should really go towards the miraculously generous boy slave and his bee carnival. When I give honey as a gift, I don't take credit for making that honey. If I had a bee colony of my own, I would individually name my bees and label that honey according to which bee shat it out as waste product, wishing I could make honey in my ass, dreaming of the day I could squeeze into a hexagon to produce something so sugary that people pay twenty dollars for a dab of it. Bees are the real celebrities on this planet.

But to turn this into a real story with real characters, would be to macerate the metaphor. The allegory is already obvious, right? People taking credit and calling themselves celebrities and failing to spread the wealth. I decided not to write that story, because Dorothy Allison said not to write in anger, that a text is better with distance between anger and the self. Let anxiety's allegory emerge in hindsight, let the metaphor sink in, glorious metaphor! I can write that angry story about the privileged class treading on the less fortunate in one word now—*Bees*. The word *bees* encapsulates it.

Every time I see a bee hovering over the jade plant in my yard from now on the metaphor will click and I will think of Babylon and my hatred of capitalism. And I hope it doesn't enrage me, I hope it doesn't, because I might take it out, accidentally, on innocent bees. I might see The Celebrity Beekeepers, instead, when I look at those black and yellow buzzbots.

See? It's already happening, I can't look at bees anymore. Whatever, it's for the best because I'm allergic to bees. I was trying to find a way to hate bees anyway. It was torture loving something that could kill me. Not like loving something that can kill me is a new concept, but bees, before this very moment, this turning point, embodied my self-destructive force. I haven't had the wherewithal to dual with my self-destructive force in any complete way, but that's another story. The sad story, right here right now, is that I suddenly detest bees, they remind me of the snooty women who will try to steal their honey, The Celebrity Beekeepers, those proprietary madames who claim ownership of bees underhandedly, who humiliate bees into submission. Don't even get me started on this, I hate bees so much now. I despise bees because of their symbolic affiliation with potential enslavement. Though, I have that potential too, that potential to be enslaved. Does that mean I have to hate myself as well?

BRONX SQUIRRELS

The black squirrels are fighting the gray squirrels in the park today, pouncing each other like royal alligators in the Roman dungeon. Red and yellow leaves trickle down like victory wreaths onto the squirrels' heads in this neighborhood where gay men dare not roam, where my lover almost got his ass kicked for wanting to wear a dress, where a tranny only blocks away got a baseball bat shoved up his ass. Maybe the black squirrels own the park just like their thuggish brothers own the block? I am not referring to those humans willing to see through color and gender, but the thugs. That's fine with me; the thugs can have this place. Black squirrels deserve territory just as much as those who connote *classic squirrel. If Squirrel was a crayon color*, the thug squirrels ask, *do you think it would be black?* No. *It would be the embarrassing Classic Gray Squirrel hue.* These problems still exist. But I'm not here to teach squirrels about crayons. They draw brilliantly in dirt with their dainty hands. I understand the phrase *going nuts* better today than ever: it's about fall, squirrel war season, it's about race wars and queer wars, frantically burying nuts under trees, those leafy allies.

Squirrels, I am here today to tell you that I do not wish to fight anymore. My dog stares at me with one eye. The other was poked out on a branch while hiking. The animals surrounding me are frazzled and haggard. I have recruited my dog to perform one last guard job in this neighborhood where crack and junk rule. My neighbor, whose apartment door is two feet from mine, deals to the local toothless citizens. His two pit bulls fight, so he keeps them in separate rooms. I often hear them tearing each other apart. Squirrels, how do you expect to survive winter when you're excluding each other according to fur color? Shouldn't you be banding together to form a furry rainbow flag?

I know, I know, the world is not ideal. Every squirrel for him or herself, cruel nature… This morning, I surrender.

I'm not telling you, squirrels, to give up fighting and sacrifice your stash for the good of your species, to starve to death so that the other colored squirrels can take over, to find hippie peace pre-winter instead of a nut. I don't want to see one more emaciated creature around here. Black squirrels, I love you. I'm fighting off despair too, while you wage warfare to secure nourishment. To be queer in this neighborhood is a beat-down. The destitution here is terrible. I wish a helicopter of money would hover over my building and rain cash so the tenants would stop feuding on their cell phones about unpaid bills. All that has rained down upon my dog and I so far is chicken bones, after one day someone munched greasy meat on the sixth floor.

It's difficult for me not to pity this one bony woman who solicits my neighbor. She has a deformed hand that she hides under a too-long trenchcoat sleeve, and loves my one-eyed dog for his related lack. *At least he is not a junky*, I want to tell her, but she stares at me vacantly, smiling with her front teeth gone, saving her remaining eye contact energy for the dog. *Hello hello*, she coos to my dog in our elevator going down, stroking his red fur, *aren't you a sweet thing.* She exists on an animal wavelength, and in that, her and I are alike.

ESCALATOR INTO THE GANGES

The trail to the escalator is lined with pigeon entrails, from diseased city birds that were gutted by Bengali tigers. *The tiger population has increased*, I read in a guidebook, *due to their eating of rock doves. These ferocious cats have extended their range north of the Ganges Delta where previously they had faced extinction.* I am not afraid of cats or avian innards, and I march right over these intestines that look like curly fries cross-bred with raw shrimp. Slippery! I am not the kind of person who flies over revolting stuff; I get right down in the shit and wade through it like a devotee.

Don't go, don't go, shout the street people loitering at the locked gate leading down to a broken escalator that dead-ends in the rushing mother river. (This river motif won't leave me alone, I'm telling you, once you get the bite the infection spreads.) The mother river, the mighty Ganges, where the ashes of the dead are scattered to reincarnate, what happens if you ride an escalator into its churning maw while still alive? Will I become that phantasmic freshwater pearl? A thyme bush, a bower bird, a toothache, a Christmas light bulb, or a garden gnome? Paneer or a metal bucket those women adjacent to the chapati vendor are scrubbing their laundry in on the other shore? What will become of me? The escalator descends into something as treacherous-looking as the foam below Hoover Dam. I hope I never have to see Hoover Dam, that cement monstrosity. What kind of idiot sees the Colorado River and thinks they'd like to build a concrete condom to contain it, to squelch its orgasmic rush? I'd like to punch that guy. Anyway, I channel the Bengali tigers, feeling refreshed and encouraged and ready to sacrifice myself after predatory cats have sniffed the same river's shore grass. Each of their whiskers is pencil-sized and each paw is the size of my front door at home, back in the USSR, a frigid place I'm done with.

I bought the travel guide and a one-way ticket, had enough with wearing leg warmers as hats and weaving old t-shirts into shirts that look country-maiden festive, like I went berserk in a strawberry patch. I'd found myself sucking lemons too frequently and mooning neighbors for cheap thrills, and I knew it was time to hurtle myself into the mother to toss a coin in the nature church's collections plate. The wisteria vine, the clown balloon, the white candle back home, it all smacked of ritual in a really faux way. It all smacked of going down on a woman I met stoned in a club when the real woman is a sumptuous river. The Ganges, suddenly, was the woman I really wanted to go down on. To think she has enormous fish doing flips in her whitewater makes me twinkle. I'm so there, what am I waiting for, lamely jogging the same Soviet block daily, running around like a beheaded chicken, there are more important things to be doing like worshipping a water goddess whose currents pump with a velocity a thousand times mine. I did the math and packed my bags.

Ma, the first word, I sip hot tea and take a whiff of that inescapable incense burning everywhere I look. Over there, a man pulls a business suit over his swami gear like the American superhero Clark Kent. Over here, ten dogs form a hump line, each mounting the last in a canine sex chain-gang. A lotus-shaped paper lantern drifts towards the rapids until a green kingfisher swoops down and flies it back to his mangrove branch. Holy moly, is that a pygmy hippo on the other beach? That was at the top of my list of things to see before I die. The escalator is broken so it's more like stairs whose crevices are slimed with algae. Algae is the same as me. I'm a drop of water on a mega wet trip, and in three minutes I'll be part mammoth aquifer.

Before I left Minsk, I took a field trip with two girlfriends to a waterslide park where we took saunas between vodka shots at the pool bar. Obese, hairy men in speedos lounged in the artificial sun under silk palm trees belying the cruel winter outside. Minus twenty it was, as we ice-skated home in our van, past the onion dome and back past the half-timber house that is now a wolf sanctuary. My beaver fur coat insulated me, preserving what body heat I'd derived from steaming and swimming in sizzling pools all day. I remember feeling like a seal and wondering—see? I'm telling you it's a water obsession—how it would feel to surf glacial floes in a cold ocean. Will frozen saltwater paralyze you? Then, my sister called and confessed her fear of fountains, not drinking fountains but the kind synchronized swimmers undulate through in Busby Berkeley films. We're both Pisces. I warned her against watching Kenneth Anger's *L'Eau D'Artifice*, that salacious film *du nuit*, because it's a fifteen-minute classical cum shot starring fountains in a French *jardin*. I hung up. I put the film on, located my oyster, and reconnoitered the lower half of my body with the day's watery glory in mind. It was then that I grasped my true need to return to primordial sludge. Mudpuppies scare me stiff but only because I know in the seat of my soul that I'll be pulling a reverse maneuver, losing my legs, right about now.

SCARLET GILIA

The cinderally was one enormous coke-can cock fest, men tearing the sides of the volcano up in their off-road vehicles, skimming the scabby, red-black scree for a trophy and a fuck in a truck bed after the race. It is an antique activity, the cinderally; I met a man nostalgic for it as we gazed at the majestic volcano across the valley from our scenic view pullout in Arizona. It was real, defacing the volcano that the Hopi consider the center of their universe. How amazing—that disparity—two variant life-styles on the side of that pointy black hill over there that looks like a shadow, a silhouette.

In the past, if a fellow like that would have told me about how he longed for the re-legalization of cinderallies, I would have launched a rocket at his crotch or at least cursed him privately when I got home, made a little voodoo doll and poked its testicles on his behalf. But this time, I took a wider view, the volcano was framed in a panoramic vista and I wanted to be strong like the volcano more than lowly like him, so I borrowed its panorama during that moment of opinion. Cut my judgment and opted for removed annotation: a piecing together of a complex societal puzzle, a man and his loser redneck friends destroying multiple rare crops of my favorite endemic wildflower, the scarlet gilia, plus the Hopi fighting for protection of the site where the first katchina was born. Here I am in the middle, mining the collision in the 21st century. It makes me weepy often enough; it used to make me so sorry for the Hopi that I felt like stabbing my eyeballs out because I am white, part of the colonial race who fucked them over, a member of the race they most despise. But pity is derogatory. I am in my car parked next to this trailer trash, not privy to friendship with a member of the Hopi hummingbird clan. I should be sacrificing myself to that volcano, throwing myself into its cone—that is how I felt ten years ago.

But this time the volcano's endurance bolsters me. It is still kicking ass before and after humanity, and that is what brings a tear to my eye this time. The volcano weathered cinderallies, and nevertheless I had just been on its trail, now part of a national park, and had photographed a magnificent crop of scarlet gilia, the brightest crop I've ever seen, a wondrous fuschia flower that I had discovered on my way to a powwow as a teenager. That flower blooms only in black lava flow, that flower that grows out of destruction is God, hands down. That is God for me. That wildflower.

We are not in an age where we can afford to tiptoe around, making conceptual art and literature that's exclusively for white intellectuals because political art is out of style; it has never been out of style and if you thought it was, effete critics, well it's back in style starting now! I don't know where these elitists have been hanging out but on the side of this volcano communities ruminate and that is politically demanding of identity art and literature. Both the Cowboys who used to destroy volcanoes on their motorcycles and their Indian enemies are unemployed and missing what they used to have; there is a lot of loss going on. I will take a position, stake it out, and make art about what I love. Why am I writing and What change do I wish to enact? What is art and What is love? Don't be shy about it, I tell myself, be direct, act with intention, be a volcanic eruption, a fury. I don't want to make characters, I want to speak directly to you.

Some critics claim that first person autobiographical voice is not fiction or that it is fiction's weakest form, but I say that is a tired battle, I say I can use whatever point of view I feel like and call it fiction. Am I emphatic about this because I am a woman? Who cares, everyone I care about is part man part woman, everyone I care about is part queer, everyone I admire cares about love first and foremost, nobody but me knows if the volcano story is true or false and you know what? Who cares? What I care about is the message I am sending out to my people. That this story's residual symbols square with what I believe. I am tired of people telling me that I need fictional characters in my fiction and that to speak directly to you, reader, from my first person female point of view is inferior. Who are you to tell me I am not inventing the best fictional character right now as I speak? You don't know me or own my voice. I tell people off, then apologize. I take license to change the approach. That is a fiction, no it's not, yes it is, who are you to say?

I live for Arizona crash-pad days like that, when stuff explodes and I can watch it crumble. It's not fun or pretty but it's real, that cinderally rider was real, he was a nice man, and the Hopi bean dance is real too, I just missed it, the Hopi are still out there, ruling the desert. I love my country, I am a patriot who spends half her life on cross-country road trips, I have crushes on everyone on a daily basis, the men and women who extrude conflict, a little more comprehension everyday, some minute intelligence, it's what I live for. I am so far from being anti-intellectual it's not even funny. This is totally fiction and it's real too. Fake fiction is fiction that's forgotten fiction and poetry are siblings.

I had another experience on a volcano, Picaya in Guatemala. I hiked it at twilight led by a short, dark-skinned man who went barefoot. He didn't give me a flashlight until I was sliding down igneous rock in the dark; I couldn't make out ground from sky, it was so black. But from the top, as six of us watched the sun go down, the sky went William Blake and I bawled then, too, for the terrifying beauty of disorientation. I didn't know how we'd get down the hill as night fell, the ground around us was puffing and smoking; I anticipated asphyxiating on sulfuric air. Veins of flowing lava around my feet. That volcano was the fixed winner in a boxing match, my flashlight was pathetic shining into lava rivers, their light so powerful, I would have tossed my flashlight in to watch its metal melt. If I made it down, I cried, it will only be because the volcano granted me permission; volcanoes are essentially control freaks. Picaya was why I was able to laugh along with the man's cinderally memory: I could relate. In one way, yes, one could tear it up all over a volcanic peak and the volcano will obviously reign supreme. Yes, I can see where he got that idea, I chortled as we worshipped the volcano, commemorated our experiences on it, mine with the flowers and his with motorcycles. Then I felt nauseous, for nothing is indestructible, even hardcore forces need a buttress, some talismanic appreciation. The barefoot man on Picaya had it right, walking barefoot on those pebbles, cutting his feet up. He was so bloody by the end of the walk, once he felt the soft rainforest's floor that night, he was hurting. Years later, I realized that was sacrifice, his pain was Picaya love. My memory of these experiences hurts, my love for writing hurts, I want to share everything with you so much. If it doesn't hurt, I'm lost.

ACKNOWLEDGMENTS

The Dad stories, though fictional, are in loving memory of Rodney Dalton and Lane Greene. "The Perverted Hobo" is for Benjamin, and "War Foods" is after Lynne's essay, "An Impossible Man." "Escape Mushroom Style" was inspired by a Chinese restaurant menu courtesy Takeshi, and the Ling Chih identification borrows copy from the *National Audubon Field Guide to North American Mushrooms*, by Gary Lincoff. "The Sad Drag Monologues" are for Stanya and Ariana.

"Small Time Spender" borrows lyrics from the song, "Super Cool Brother" by LA Bare Faxx, and "Jackpot (II)" borrows the Lady'chete from Kathy. "Treehouses" in "Word Salad" was inspired by Jim. Gratitude to my animal companions, Yucca and Shuggie. To Amy, Eileen, Dennis, Bjorn, Sadie, Jesse, Bianca, Sierra, Gail, Francine, Heidi, Jay, Andrea, and Sue: thank you for your inspirational friendship, art, support, and conversation that led to ideas spawning the invented characters here. Thanks to NYU, Pratt, and Vermont College of Fine Arts, Sumanth Prubhaker of Madras Press, Dan Nadel of Picturebox, the CANADA gallery crew. Thanks to my family: Tammie, Greg, Sunny, Amanda, as well as Mike and KC, brothers from another mother. Thanks to Xylor for the cover image. Thanks to Sean for reading early drafts. Thanks to Eric and Eliza for publishing *Baby Geisha* and for making me excited about the future of books. This book {in spirit} is dedicated to Stevie Wonder, and {in physical reality} is dedicated to Matt: true love, talented artist, dedicated editor and muse.

About the cover art

FLASK, by Xylor Jane

"Flask" is the third mate in Moby Dick, and the title of the drawing. Xylor Jane was born on a palindrome 12/21, the longest night of the year. A double 7, cat and candy lover, looking to take harmonica lessons. She is represented by CANADA Gallery in New York. Her work has been exhibited internationally and can be viewed in her most recent catalogue, Xylor Jane (Picturebox).

Also published by **TWO DOLLAR RADIO**

THE CORRESPONDENCE ARTIST

A NOVEL BY BARBARA BROWNING

A Trade Paperback Original; 978-0-9820151-9-3; $16 US

"A deft look at modern life that's both witty and devastating."
—*Nylon*

Vivian has been carrying on a love affair with a famous artist. Rather than revealing her paramour's identity, she creates a series of fictional lovers in the service of telling her tale.

THE PEOPLE WHO WATCHED HER PASS BY

A NOVEL BY SCOTT BRADFIELD

A Trade Paperback Original; 978-0-9820151-5-5; $14.50 US

"A billowy adventure of a book."
—*New York Times Book Review*

Salome Jensen is a three-year-old girl whose drift across America inspires a perspective of the world and an understanding of its people more meaningful than the most erudite observer could muster.

THE ORANGE EATS CREEPS

A NOVEL BY GRACE KRILANOVICH

A Trade Paperback Original; 978-0-9820151-8-6; $16 US

- ✱ National Book Foundation 2010 '5 Under 35' Selection.
- ✱ *NPR* Best Books of 2010.
- ✱ *The Believer* Book Award Finalist.

"Krilanovich's work will make you believe that new ways of storytelling are still emerging from the margins." —*NPR*

A girl with drug-induced ESP and an eerie connection to Patty Reed, searches for her disappeared foster sister along 'The Highway That Eats People.'

Also published by TWO DOLLAR RADIO

THE DROP EDGE OF YONDER

A NOVEL BY RUDOLPH WURLITZER

A Trade Paperback Original; 978-0-9763895-5-2; $15.00 US

* *Time Out New York*'s #1 Best Book of 2008.
* *ForeWord* Magazine 2008 Gold Medal in Literary Fiction.

"The most hallucinogenic western you'll ever catch in the moviehouse of your mind's eye." —*Bookforum*

A new contemporary classic that follows Zebulon Shook as he explores America's true myth of origins.

FLATS / QUAKE

TWO CLASSIC NOVELS BY RUDOLPH WURLITZER

Trade Paperback; 978-0-9820151-4-8; $17 US

"Together they provide a tour of the dissolution of identity that was daily life in the sixties."
—Michael Silverblatt, *KCRW's Bookworm*

Flats is a post-apocalyptic exploration of the human self. *Quake* chronicles the unraveling of society after an earthquake strikes Los Angeles. Both are nihilistic and haunting, as well as uncomfortably foreboding.

NOG

A NOVEL BY RUDOLPH WURLITZER

A Trade Paperback Original; 978-0-9820151-2-4; $15.50 US

"[*Nog*'s] combo of Samuel Beckett syntax and hippie-era freakiness mapped out new literary territory for generations to come."
—*Time Out New York*

In Wurlitzer's hypnotic voice, *Nog* tells the tale of a man adrift through the American West, armed with nothing more than three pencil-thin memories and an octopus in a bathysphere.

THE CAVE MAN
A NOVEL BY XIAODA XIAO
A Trade Paperback Original; 978-0-9820151-3-1; $15.50 US

"As a parable of modern China, [*The Cave Man*] is chilling."
—*Boston Globe*

An extraordinary and moving portrait of a man brutalized in Mao's China.

THE VISITING SUIT
A MEMOIR BY XIAODA XIAO
A Trade Paperback Original; 978-0-9820151-7-9; $16.50 US

"These stories personify the compassion, humor, and dignity inherent not just in survival but in triumphing over despair." —*O: The Oprah Magazine*

When Xiaoda Xiao was twenty-years-old he tore a poster of Mao. Without a trail he was sentenced to five years in labor prison. A poignant and incredibly moving memoir-in-stories.

YOU ARE MY HEART AND OTHER STORIES
STORIES BY JAY NEUGEBOREN
A Trade Paperback Original; 978-0-9826848-8-7; $16 US

"[Neugeboren] might not be as famous as some of his compeers, like Philip Roth or John Updike, but it's becoming increasingly harder to argue that he's any less talented."
—*Kirkus Reviews*

From the secluded villages in the south of France, to the cattle crawl in the Valley of a Thousand Hills in South Africa, Neugeboren examines the great mysteries that unsettle human relationships.

Also published by **TWO DOLLAR RADIO**

SEVEN DAYS IN RIO
A NOVEL BY FRANCIS LEVY
A Trade Paperback Original; 978-0-9826848-7-0; $16 US

"The funniest American novel since Sam Lipsyte's *The Ask*."
—*Village Voice*

Kenny Cantor is a CPA and sex-tourist who becomes waylaid at a psychoanalytic conference in this wicked satire.

EROTOMANIA: A ROMANCE
A NOVEL BY FRANCIS LEVY
A Trade Paperback Original; 978-0-9763895-7-6; $14 US
* *Inland Empire Weekly* Standout Book of 2008.
* *Queerty.com* Top 10 Book of 2008.

"Levy is our generation's D.H. Lawrence, Henry Miller, and Charles Bukowski rolled into one."
—*Inland Empire Weekly*

A comedic, absurdist portrait of a modern-day romance.

THE SHANGHAI GESTURE
A NOVEL BY GARY INDIANA
A Trade Paperback Original; 978-0-9820151-0-0; $15.50 US

"[Gary Indiana] is the primary reporter of the underground, the dissociation of cultures, the new behaviors; there is a sense that if you want to understand what has happened in America, you would have to read Gary Indiana. And this newest book is a leap forward." —Michael Silverblatt, *KCRW*'s *Bookworm*

Indiana applies his prickly wit, nihilistic vision, and utterly original voice to this side-splitting spin on Fu Manchu.